Just Listen

OTHER BOOKS BY
JEFF VANOUDENHOVE

THE DARK SERIES:

Book 1 - DARK PLACE

Book 2 - DARK LANE

Book 3 - DARK QUEEN

Book 4 - DARK CHILD

Book 5 - THE FINAL DARK

SCREAMS IN THE DARK AND OTHER TWISTED TALES

THE ALPHABET KILLER

For signed copies of the author's books, please visit:

javo-publication.square.site

Just Listen

JEFF VANOUDENHOVE

JAVO
PUBLICATION

Westfield, MA

JAVO Publication
Westfield, Massachusetts 01085

This is a work of fiction. The characters, places, and events portrayed in this book are either the product of the author's imagination or are used fictitiously. Any similarity to real persons, living or dead, business establishments, or events is coincidental and not intended by the author.

ISBN: 979-8-9865975-5-3

Library of Congress Control Number: 2024902024

Cover design by Jeff VanOudenhove

For Loni
A devoted fan whose encouraging words made
this all worthwhile

Acknowledgments

Writing is not always an easy task. When I start the adventure of a new book, it is very rough and needs much smoothing out. Because of that, I am so very grateful for the relationship I have with my editor, Elizabeth Kelly. She is detailed and thorough, yet not forceful with her demands about overall content. She is flexible and understanding with what I am trying to convey in my stories. She tweaks, she pokes, she prods, but in the end, the story is still mine to shape and mold how I see fit. The result is a much better story than what it would have been had I not had her guidance and dedication to smooth out those rough edges. I am so very thankful.

I'd also like to thank Dave Whiteley, who offered insight into the world of a forensic psychiatric hospital. His knowledge and advice were invaluable in helping me understand the inner workings of what goes on within those walls.

My acknowledgments wouldn't be complete if I didn't thank members of the Whip City Wordsmiths for critiquing my work and offering encouragement, and to the members of the Psychological Thriller Readers group on Facebook for their wonderful support and kind words.

And finally, to fans of my work, those who this and all of my stories are for. I couldn't, nor would I want to, do this alone. Thank you all.

On to the next.

Blank Page

Who will tell my story, Sylvie thought, looking down at a runaway strand of her long brown hair that had fallen from her head and draped itself across the half-written, lined page of her notebook. She didn't usually let her thoughts wander when with a patient, but after Greta's unsavory comment, it just got away from her. *But really*, she thought, *who would want to tell my story?*

"Did you hear me?" Greta shouted, snapping Sylvie back to her duties. "I didn't ask you to write down my life story, for fuck's sake. I better not see that shit on Dateline or something."

Sylvie displayed a half-hearted smile, trying to disguise her discomfort.

"Yes, Greta," Sylvie replied calmly, her voice soft and controlled, "I heard you. Did you feel you needed to shout just then?"

"As a matter of fact, I did," Greta responded. "It's what happens when you look at me with that dumb, glossed-over stare of yours. You sit there with your pretty eyes, your pretty smile, flashing those dimples of yours, thinking you know me, and writing down all kinds of shit about me. Maybe I don't want my story told. Did you think of that?"

Pretty eyes? Sylvie thought, disregarding the rest of the woman's rant. They were just a bland hazel. Plain. Run of the mill. Nothing compared to the vibrant blue of the woman's sitting across from her. Coming from Greta, however, she'd take the compliment.

The older woman had no qualms about speaking her mind. At seventy-one years old, she figured she didn't have much time left to tell everybody what she thought of them. If the woman didn't like you, you'd be the first to know. If she *did* like you, well, you'd be the first. At that moment, however, Greta's outspoken demeanor wasn't uncalled for since Sylvie let her professionalism noticeably slip.

"I do apologize, Greta," Sylvie ceded, brushing the stray hair from her notebook and bringing her full attention back to the elderly woman. "Why wouldn't you want your story told?"

"Why wouldn't *you* want your story told?" Greta returned, the question an obvious ploy to keep from having to answer.

"This isn't about me," Sylvie replied. "This is about you releasing the past that still has a hold on you. Eventually, I hope you'll feel comfortable enough to discuss what happened. I'm sure it's a fascinating story."

"Fascinating to *you*, maybe," Greta snarled, turning her bright blue eyes away in disgust. "Besides, it sounds like you already know everything there is to know."

"I've read your file, yes," Sylvie nodded. "That doesn't give me the full story. That doesn't tell me who the real Greta Lambeau is. I'd like to hear about it from you. In your own words. What do you say? I think it would do you some good to share."

The gray-haired woman turned her stare back, her eyes narrow and filled with disdain.

"It didn't do me any good to share when it first happened, did it?" Greta snapped.

"Well, I don't know," Sylvie responded, startled by the woman's response. "It might have done you some good. Perhaps, if you *didn't* share back then, things might be worse for you today."

"Worse than being in this shithole?" Greta questioned, throwing her hands up to acknowledge her surroundings. "I don't think so."

Patients like Greta were commonplace at the "shithole" known as Somerset Psychiatric Institution for the Criminally Insane. It was a small psychiatric facility in central New Jersey, housing less than fifty patients, once run by the Department of

Corrections. The building and surrounding property were later sold to the Department of Mental Health, which updated the facility's gloomy interior to better resemble that of a hospital instead of a place of incarceration - though many of Somerset's long-term patients seemed content with referring to themselves as "prisoners." As part of the state's massive overhaul, most of the detention-style doors and locked entryways were removed and replaced with less intimidating electronic entrances requiring badge scanners. Due to the hospital's unique layout, however, some steel doors oddly remained as a secondary security measure to prevent patients from leaving the ward unattended. In addition, unapproachable and often menacing prison guards were relieved of their duties in favor of hiring security guards who were more friendly and personable.

Greta Lambeau had been a resident of the psychiatric hospital long enough to experience both worlds. If Somerset was a "shithole," Sylvie shuddered to think what it was like before.

The doctor displayed a hint of an encouraging smile, "Our current setting aside, I think you know this was for the best."

"Why?" Greta hurled another dirty glance, "So I can talk to a smart-ass, know-it-all therapist once a week? I never said I needed help, and I sure don't need some young, fresh-faced kid telling me I do."

Sylvie gritted her teeth behind closed lips so she wouldn't give away her emotions. She stared quietly to gather herself, breathing deeply before casually shifting her eyes to the clock on the far wall. She felt a twinge of guilt for being relieved at its display.

"Well then, Greta," Sylvie responded, "you'll be happy to know our time is up."

She closed the notepad on her lap and stood from the barely cushioned metal chair, thankful the session was over. Swinging the pages under her arm, Sylvie glared across from her and curled her lip before responding.

"And we've been over this, Greta. I'm hardly a 'kid.' I'm thirty-eight. That may seem young to you, but I'm an adult. I'm also not a therapist. I'm a qualified clinical psychologist. That means I'm a doctor just like Dr. Prichard, even if you don't care to acknowledge me as such."

She stared down at the seventy-one-year-old, whose unnerving silence spoke volumes.

"Greta, I know you don't like these sessions, but we must have them. Let's try to be productive, shall we?"

Without waiting for a response or even a hateful glare, Sylvie turned away. She knew it wasn't professional, but it sure felt good to get that off her chest. The staff was quick to respond, already heading in her direction to collect Greta and assist her back to her room.

Maybe, Sylvie thought, *the aged woman would reflect on her words*. If not, there was always the following week. But for now, whether she wanted to or not, Sylvie would do her own reflecting as she walked away, hearing Greta's previously spoken words in her head.

"I didn't ask you to write down my life story."

No life story written today, she thought; *perhaps another time.* Sadly, Sylvie felt similarly frustrated about her own life. What was there to tell? A never-been-married workaholic, spending her days listening to those with mental health disorders, trying to solve all their problems. She knew she couldn't save them all, but in her brief, six-year career, having delayed her continuing education until later in life due to personal issues, she still remained hopeful. But perhaps, saving everyone else wasn't what she needed. Maybe she needed only to save herself.

Who will tell my story? Sylvie thought. *Who would want to tell my story?* After all, there wasn't anything special to tell; just another handful of blank pages.

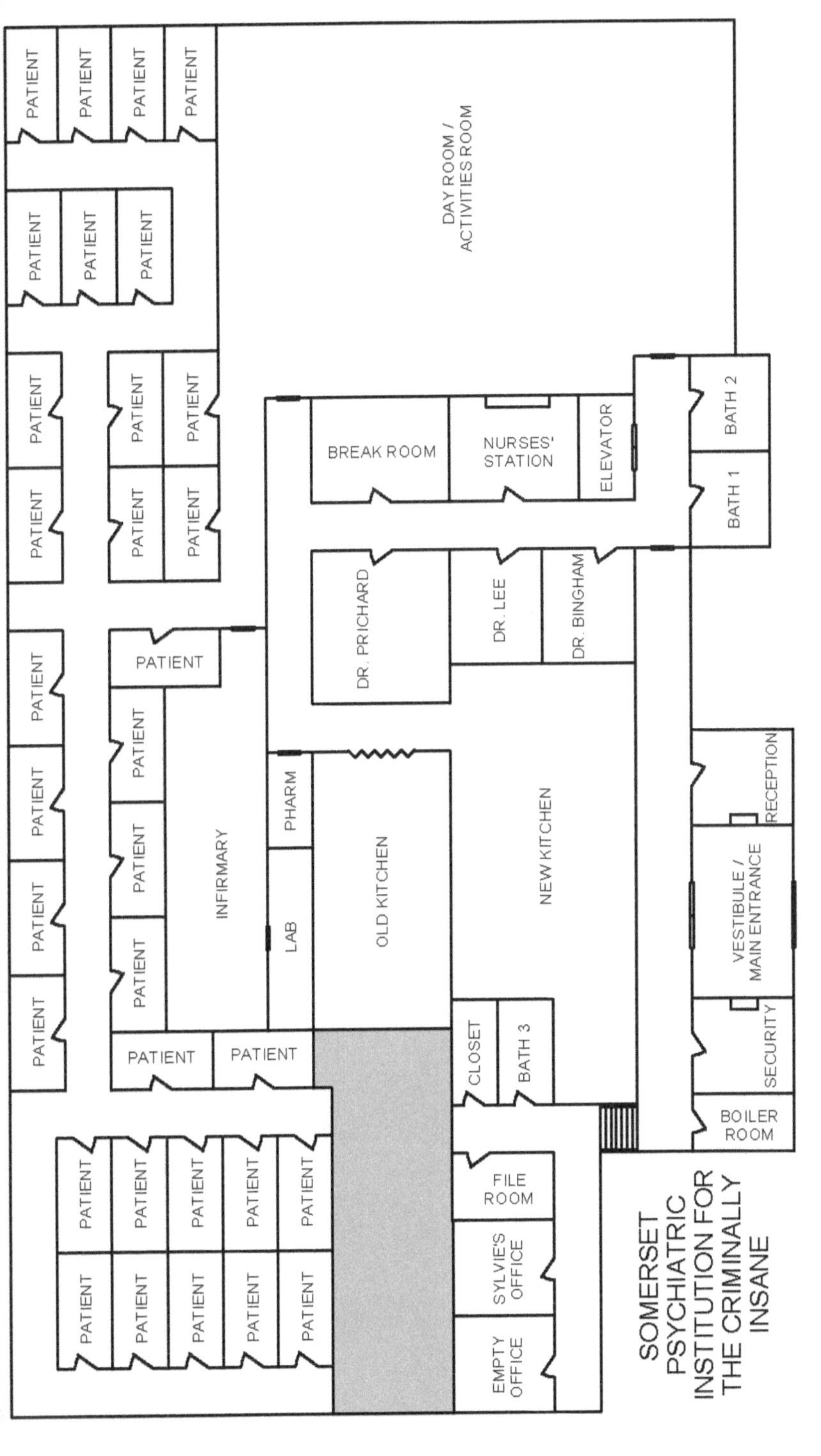

PATIENT
PATIENT
PATIENT
PATIENT
PATIENT
PATIENT
PATIENT
PATIENT
PATIENT
PATIENT
PATIENT
PATIENT
DAY ROOM / ACTIVITIES ROOM
BREAK ROOM
NURSES' STATION
ELEVATOR
BATH 2
BATH 1
DR. PRICHARD
DR. LEE
DR. BINGHAM
PATIENT
PATIENT
PATIENT
PATIENT
PATIENT
INFIRMARY
PHARM
LAB
OLD KITCHEN
NEW KITCHEN
RECEPTION
VESTIBULE / MAIN ENTRANCE
SECURITY
BOILER ROOM
PATIENT
PATIENT
CLOSET
BATH 3
PATIENT
PATIENT
PATIENT
PATIENT
PATIENT
PATIENT
PATIENT
PATIENT
PATIENT
PATIENT
FILE ROOM
SYLVIE'S OFFICE
EMPTY OFFICE
SOMERSET PSYCHIATRIC INSTITUTION FOR THE CRIMINALLY INSANE

Chapter 1

Safe Secrets

The dimly lit lamp beside Sylvie's bed provided enough light to see the words on the page, but it could never shine bright enough to illuminate the meaning behind them. She spent most of her evenings combing through the various files of the hospital's patients, wondering if her work was even making a difference in their lives. She wanted to believe so, but it was getting harder each day. Patients like Greta Lambeau did nothing to help relieve such doubts.

Greta wasn't even the worst patient Sylvie had (that distinction fell upon that perverted lech, Roger Loomis, with the way he flapped his tongue in a sexually suggestive manner anytime she was near). No, Greta wasn't the worst patient, she was just the one holding onto the most secrets, and no matter what textbook strategies Sylvie employed to get the woman to open up, Greta held onto those secrets tighter than a frog's ass.

Sure, the older woman had stated on numerous occasions that she once told her story, and all it ever got her was misery and grief, but there's no record of what she shared, and nobody around to corroborate whether she did or not. It was often difficult to take her at her word since she had been caught in quite a few lies during her lengthy stay, but Sylvie believed there was something in the woman's past that triggered her mental breakdown, and if she could only tear down the fortified wall Greta had constructed, perhaps it was also something that held the key to her recovery. All the late-night speculations weighed heavily on Sylvie's mind, yet she was no closer to unraveling the mystery that was Greta Lambeau. Sylvie knew she couldn't force the woman to open up, but she believed she could help her if only she could pierce the patient's impenetrable defenses.

Shaking her head in frustration while her eyes grew unbearably heavy, Sylvie scanned the folders scattered across her bed. She'd awoken many mornings with the files still draped over her as a secondary blanket, papers strewn about in chaotic disarray, a sign of the previous night's restlessness. She wouldn't let that happen this evening; she was well aware of her propensity to drift off soon after her head hit the pillow, though, at the moment, her head rested against the wood frame of the headboard while the pillow lay under her lower back for support.

She gathered the cluttered folders, compiling them into a messy stack, then tamped them on the mattress beside her to straighten them. She could live with the occasional accidental untidiness if she dozed off, but that didn't stop her from trying to be somewhat organized while still awake.

The folders will still be here in the morning, she thought, placing them on her nightstand. *The patients will still require my help. Why should I lose sleep over it?* And, with that thought, Sylvie flipped the switch on the lamp's base and slid herself deeper into the blanket, thankful to be reclaiming her thoughts away from work and allowing her head to settle into the extra-soft pillow that was eager to take her away for the night.

Sylvie's eyes snapped open at what she thought was the sudden sound of a chair scraping across the kitchen's tile floor. She lay silent, her head still fixed within the pillow's fibers, listening for something other than her shallow breaths. Her eyes focused first on the closed door of the room, staring at the small gap between it and the floor, searching for any indication of moving shadows where they shouldn't belong. After a moment's passing with no further disturbance, Sylvie's eyes shifted to the clock on her nightstand, the glowing numbers showing she still had seventeen minutes before its annoying buzz demanded her awakening. Feeling her heart slowly sink back into her chest after realizing how easily dreams could play tricks on one's senses, she let her shoulders relax, then closed her eyes, hoping to take advantage of the remaining seventeen minutes at her disposal.

She would have fallen back asleep in minutes had it not been for the second sound of a sliding chair, forcing her to abruptly throw the blankets aside as she sat up to be more alert. Her heart pounding, Sylvie slid her legs off the bed, placing them gently on the wood floor, trying to keep from making any noises herself. She knew where all the creaks in the floorboards were, but with her nerves shooting chills through her body, she hoped she could keep it together enough to avoid them as she pushed herself upright. Sliding her right foot forward, she felt a slight draft creep up the leg of her pajama pants which, together with her heightened nerves, caused her to shiver.

Sylvie knew it was doing her no good taking her time getting to the door. If somebody wanted in, they had only to turn the knob to gain entry. That thought suddenly jolted her "fight or flight" response, and she opted for "fight." Springing forward, she ignored the loud squeaks erupting from the floor and pressed her back against the door.

"Who's there?" she shouted. "I'm dialing the police."

A second of silence crawled by, making it feel more like an hour, before a young voice softly replied, "It's me, Sylvie."

With those three little words, all the fear Sylvie felt immediately faded. The voice was Kevin's.

Kevin Messier was a young teenage boy, thirteen or fourteen – Sylvie'd forgotten which exactly - who lived down the street. He was always looking for chores and odd jobs to do for his neighbors so he could earn a little spending money. Sylvie took an immediate liking to the boy, not because he was willing to work for what he wanted, though it was a refreshing change from most of the younger generation who had everything handed to them. Instead, it was because she could tell something troubled the often brooding young boy, and her instinct to want to solve everyone's problems, even those who were not her patients, kicked in. She was never intrusive when speaking with Kevin, instead merely offering a sympathetic ear anytime the boy felt he needed to talk. It wasn't often teenagers willingly opened up to strangers, a not-so-subtle indication that Kevin's problems may have been a bit, well, no pun intended, messier than most others his age.

With her anxiety now abated, Sylvie gripped the doorknob and slowly exited the bedroom, wondering what this early-morning intrusion could be about. Shaking her head, she entered the kitchen to find Kevin sitting at the table, his head heavily propped in his left hand while his right hand fidgeted with a salt shaker. He made no attempt to acknowledge her presence, content in simply watching the shaker spin under his fingers.

"Kevin," she stated calmly, holding back whatever frustration she felt, "what are you doing here? How did you get in?"

Kevin shifted his eyes upward, staring at Sylvie, whose hands were on her hips, telling of her annoyance.

"The key under your mat," Kevin replied, throwing his thumb over his shoulder toward the side door. "I didn't mean to scare you," he continued. "I knocked a couple of times, but you didn't answer. I thought you might be asleep, so I just figured I'd wait in here until you were awake. I'm sorry," he said, standing from his chair, "I'll go."

"Hold on, Kevin," Sylvie responded, placing her hand on his shoulder. "I didn't say you had to leave; I was just surprised you were here at such an early hour. What's going on?" Her thoughts drifted to relocating her key.

"Nothing," he replied, sitting back down and letting his arms drop to his lap. "I just didn't feel like being at home."

"So then, nothing going on you needed to talk about?" Sylvie inquired, unconvinced. "I mean, something must've brought you here."

The boy remained silent, his chin to his chest and shaking his head. Sylvie didn't need a degree in psychology to know something was amiss with the boy, but she knew trying to pry it out of him could cause more harm than good. He needed to feel comfortable and safe. Sylvie could only offer what comfort she could. He would share when he was ready.

"Well, since you're here," she began, "how about a bowl of cereal? Oh, and next time, please ring the doorbell first so you don't scare the daylights out of me."

"Okay," the boy nodded.

Sylvie grabbed a bowl from the overhead cabinet and placed it on the table. She could see his demeanor brighten a bit as he reached forward and slid the bowl closer.

"Can I ask you something, Sylvie?" Kevin questioned while his gracious host shuffled through items in her pantry, searching for the elusive cereal she promised.

"Sure, kiddo," she replied. "Ask away."

"Dialing the police, huh?" he responded snarkily with a slight snicker.

"What's so funny about that?" Sylvie questioned, emerging from the pantry with a box of Raisin Bran.

Smirking, the boy answered, "You *do* realize I know you don't own a cell phone, right? And since your only house phone is over there on the counter..," He pointed.

"Yeah, well.., your average home invader doesn't know that, does he?" she responded, sticking out her tongue playfully. "But you make a good point; maybe I should invest in a second phone in my bedroom."

"So weird," Kevin said, smiling and filling his bowl.

"What?"

"You're the only person I know who doesn't have a cell phone."

"Oh really?" Sylvie responded, pulling the milk from the fridge. "So, where's your phone then, smarty-pants?"

"That's different," he remarked. "I'm a kid."

"I know it may seem a bit unusual to you," Sylvie countered, pouring the milk over his cereal, "but I think cell phones are a leading contributor to many of today's social communication issues." She placed the milk down by his bowl and sat across from him. "People don't know how to talk with one another anymore, and they certainly don't know how to sit back and just listen."

She was hoping her words would encourage Kevin to communicate what he was feeling at that moment, but as she watched him slip one hand under the table while his eyes shifted down from hers to focus on her loose tank top, she quickly realized what those feelings were.

Turning red with embarrassment and realizing that, with all the earlier excitement, she had neglected to put on a bra, she quickly folded her arms across her chest to curb the teenaged adolescent's surging hormones.

"I should get ready for work," she said awkwardly, swinging herself sideways in the chair. "Have another bowl if you'd like," she continued while standing and walking toward the bedroom. "I'll only be a few minutes."

Closing the bedroom door behind her, she wrestled with whether to feel offended or flattered by the boy's wandering eyes.

It shouldn't surprise me, Sylvie thought, grabbing a shirt and bra from the basket of clothes she'd been procrastinating to fold. *He's a pubescent teen at that awkward age where his body is going through changes. He didn't mean anything by it.* Brushing it off with a smirk, she shuffled into the bathroom to make herself presentable.

Several minutes later, Sylvie emerged from the bathroom, a toothbrush in her hand.

"You know, Kevin," she announced, turning the corner into the kitchen, "you should probably call your..,"

She stopped in mid-sentence once she saw the boy was gone, the half-eaten bowl of Raisin Bran still on the table. She glanced out the side door's window to see if he was still nearby. He wasn't.

Maybe he was slightly embarrassed as well, she thought. Either way, the boy had gone, and she needed to finish getting ready for work.

Kevin's rushed departure without first saying goodbye left Sylvie even more curious about his unexpected visit. She wished he had had enough courage to open up about his troubles, but he refused to let her in. She knew she could break through if given enough time, but he rarely granted it. Whatever secrets the boy was holding onto, he must've felt they were only safe with him.

Didn't we all feel that way, she thought, *about the secrets we kept?* After all, there were a few secrets she held onto herself. It was the nature of her work - the confidentiality between doctor and patient. The secrets of those she could never share were a heavy burden at times but worth the weight if it meant she could *un*burden those in her care, if only for a while. Their problems always returned (they'd never truly gone away), but for a moment, their troubles faded, and they felt relief for perhaps the first time. That's what made the job worthwhile. That was why she did what she did.

Sylvie glanced at the clock and dropped her shoulders, realizing she should focus on finishing getting herself ready if she planned to make it to work on time. She placed the toothbrush between her teeth and walked back toward the bathroom, reciting the promising phrase she'd stated every morning since her first day on the job:

"Today's going to be the day."

Chapter 2

A Lack of Faith

Sylvie tapped her fingers on her knee in a subtle rhythmic pattern, recalling the beat from the last song she had heard before arriving at the hospital. It was more from nerves than anything else, but if she could convince herself it was the music instead, it would help ease her mind.

The day was Thursday. She always felt this way on Thursdays, though she had no idea why. Kevin's morning intrusion had made her forget until she caught sight of Dr. Prichard rounding the corner from his office. It was the one day he worked rounds at the hospital, splitting the time between his private practice and serving the state. He was a tenured psychiatrist who had worked full-time at the hospital for nineteen years before branching out. Because of that, though, she wondered why the hospital allowed him to keep his cozy office - the largest among the entire staff - when it remained vacant for most of the week. They could have relocated him to one of the smaller offices along "Doctors' Row" and offered his palatial suite to someone more dedicated to the patients within the psychiatric hospital.

She wasn't thinking selfishly (though she didn't much care for the closet of an office she was relegated to on the lower floor). She just felt others were more deserving of the larger space. Dr. Lee came to mind. As the only surgeon on staff, he certainly should have been considered as the new resident of Dr. Prichard's office. Instead, his office was only slightly larger than hers, though in a much more desirable location on the main floor.

With her thoughts distracted while she waited for her next patient, she didn't hear the orderly approach from the side until his words startled her.

"Something troubling you, Miss Z?" the orderly questioned, causing Sylvie to stop tapping her knee in favor of placing her hand on her chest in alarm.

"Oh, Tremont," she gasped excitedly, turning in her chair to greet him, "it's you."

"Sorry to scare you, Miss Z," he smiled tenderly. "I promise I didn't mean it."

"I know, Tremont," she responded, dropping her hand to her leg.

Tremont Williams was the only orderly, or psychiatric attendant as they were more commonly known, who refrained from calling her "Dr. Zcieveteveicz." She didn't mind. He meant no disrespect by it. As a black man originally from Louisiana, his mother raised him to address women as either "Miss" or "Mrs." depending on their marital status. Not realizing she was a doctor when they'd first met, he'd made the mistake of addressing her as "Miss" instead of "Dr." And since he couldn't pronounce her last name anyway, even though she had sounded it out for him a few times before, *She-vet-a-vich*, she became "Miss Z." instead. The title stuck.

It wasn't lost on her that the name wasn't the easiest to pronounce. The registrars on Ellis Island probably had a field day with it after her great-grandparents first emigrated to the U.S. from Poland. Either that, or they played a nasty joke on the impoverished couple by turning what should have been a simple name into a complex palindrome, though she'd read somewhere that the practice of changing the names of the new arrivals was a myth. That was probably true. After all, if the officials had been in the habit of changing names to something easier to say, she imagined she would now be Sylvie Chevette or something similar instead.

"Nothing's troubling me, Tremont," she replied. "I was just lost in my thoughts while I waited for my next patient. How are you doing?"

"I'm doing good, Miss Z," he replied, standing motionless for a moment before shifting his eyes down to the floor and dropping his chin heavily to his chest, his normally cheery smile fading.

"Is there . . . something troubling *you*, Tremont?" Sylvie questioned, noticing his sudden change in disposition.

Tremont lifted his chin, a forced smile on his face, an obvious indication there was.

"Oh, there's no need to worry about me, Miss Z. I'm sorry to be bothering you."

"You're not bothering me at all, Tremont," she assured him. "In fact, I've got a few minutes before Roger comes out; I'd love the company if you want to chat about something." She motioned toward the empty armchair across from her. She could tell the kindly man's thoughts were distracted by something he wanted to get out.

Tremont smiled and nodded. "Well, I suppose I could sit for a couple of minutes without getting into trouble."

"Sure, you can," Sylvie responded with a smile as the psychiatric attendant walked by her to take a seat at her request.

"You're not like the other doctors," Tremont began, sitting uncomfortably statuesque in the chair, his palms gripped tightly around his knees.

"Oh? How do you mean?" Sylvie inquired.

"Well, I mean, you don't lock yourself away like the others, meeting with patients secluded in your office."

It was true her style was a bit unconventional, if only adopted to maintain her own sanity. The lower floor where her office was located was dark and dreary and hardly a location to where her patients should be escorted. Not to mention, something about being in the bowels of the hospital always made her feel uneasy, which is why she began conducting her meetings in a secluded corner of the Day Room, the general area where patients would assemble and enjoy various activities.

"And you actually *listen* to your patients," Tremont continued. "It shows, Miss Z."

Sylvie smiled appreciatively at the psych attendant's comment.

"Just as I'm listening now," she stated. "What's going on, Tremont? You seem out of sorts."

Silence overtook the next few seconds while the attendant gathered himself, wondering if he should share his vulnerabilities with the doctor. He reached up with one hand and swiped his index finger under his nose, removing a droplet of snot that had formed.

"It's my boy," he opened. "He's real sick. The doctors don't know what's wrong with him."

"Oh no, Tremont," Sylvie expressed with sullen eyes, "I'm so sorry to hear that."

Had their chairs been closer together, she would have reached forward and grabbed his hand (making sure it was the one without snot).

"My wife keeps telling me he's in the Lord's hands," Tremont continued, "and that whatever happens to our little Aaron, it's part of God's great plan. My mama raised me to be a God-fearing man, Miss Z., and I have never before questioned his intentions, but what kind of God lets an innocent child suffer like that?"

Sylvie dropped her shoulders in regret, realizing there was only so much her words could do, and they would never be enough.

"I'm afraid," Sylvie began, "I'm probably not the most qualified to speak with you regarding the subject of God and his 'great plan.' I've never been the religious type."

"But *I* have been," Tremont professed. "All my life."

"Well, there's nothing wrong with having faith in something greater than you. It's important."

"But I feel I'm losing my faith, Miss Z. I'm losing my faith in God."

"Sometimes our faith is tested when we need it the most," Sylvie responded. "But faith in any form can be a powerful thing. Have faith in the doctors and nurses in your son's care. Have faith in your wife's love. Have faith in your son's will to live. And most importantly, have faith in yourself and how strong you can be during this trying time."

Tremont's eyes began welling with tears as he tried disguising his sadness by turning his head and casually wiping them dry with the sleeve of his crisply ironed olive green shirt. He then turned back, his cheeks puffy and damp from the stray runaway tears that escaped his initial swipe, his lower lip quivering.

"Thank you, Miss Z.," he nodded. Then he pressed his lips together tightly and raised his chin pridefully. "See, I knew you was a good listener."

Without waiting for a response, Tremont slapped his palms against his thighs and stood from his chair. "I should get back to work before the other patients think *I'm* crazy too."

Sylvie cringed at his words and shook her head at him. "Not crazy, Tremont. People with mental health disorders. But I knew what you meant."

He nodded.

"And listen," she continued, "I'm always here if you need to talk. Okay? But, you might also consider speaking with a member of the clergy, as well. It seems important to you, and it might help ease some of your concerns."

"I appreciate that, Miss Z.," he answered. Then, he somberly turned and strolled toward the patients on the far side of the room who had gathered around the television, its channels limited to either the Game Show Network or old westerns.

Sylvie watched in amazement how easily Tremont repressed his pain when surrounded by others under his care. She wondered if he even realized how strong he was. She could only imagine what he and his family must be going through, and yet, if not for their brief discussion, she'd never have known. The man hid it well. She could relate.

Do any of the others know, she wondered. *Or is this yet another secret I must keep?*

She wasn't given time to ponder the unverbalized question as she heard the loudening sounds of grunts and wheezes quickly approaching. The man himself had arrived.

Roger was now in her presence.

Chapter 3

Roger Loomis

It wasn't difficult to decipher what was going through Roger Loomis' mind, his lustful stare accompanied by his salivating tongue as it swayed back and forth across his bottom lip. He'd often dangle it from his mouth like a dog in heat, occasionally forming his first two digits into a V and placing them in front of his lips while his tongue flapped suggestively between them in a disgusting display. The man was mentally ill and sexually frustrated - two things that never went well together.

Since her arrival at the hospital, Sylvie never noticed Roger pose a threat to anyone, though she knew the man to be dangerous. Perhaps it was because he was the only one of her patients whose psych attendant chaperones stayed close by, even during their discussions. She was thankful for that.

As much as she didn't like to think about it, she couldn't help but imagine what horrible things the man could do to her if the two attendants weren't present.

Roger was in his late forties and had been in and out of institutions since his teen years. Sylvie believed his issues stemmed from his early childhood, when he, at the age of five, had been repeatedly molested by his babysitter. The young woman, listed as Tabitha in his psychiatric file, was in her early twenties when she first requested her five-year-old charge accompany her into the mother's bedroom so he could help her find something she had "accidentally" dropped into her underwear. Many more times were to follow and to a much more disturbing degree.

When Roger was eight, his mother found out what Tabitha had been doing to her son but continued to let it happen for several more years since, as her confession to the police during her arrest stated, "good babysitters were hard to find."

Roger was shuffled off to a foster home where, when he was thirteen years old, he raped his ten-year-old foster sister, which landed him in a juvenile detention center until he was eighteen. Upon his release, he was fortunate enough to get a job working at Blockbuster Video for a short time until a customer noticed him fondling himself behind the counter while staring at a pre-pubescent girl. He was arrested on charges of indecent exposure and placed on the then-recently established sex offenders' list. The judge presiding over the case ruled that Roger was to undergo a psych evaluation, which was what first ensured his glorious stay at the grand resort that was the Teton Psychiatric Hospital, a much larger facility than Somerset, located in upstate New York.

Discharged six years later after convincing doctors his tendency toward lewd and sexually aberrant behavior had been suppressed, Roger was again free to reenter the world as a valuable member of society. But since the horrific events of 9/11 had taken place during his hospital stay, society had become a very different place than what he'd remembered.

It wasn't long after his release that Roger voluntarily admitted himself back into the Teton Psych Hospital, claiming he couldn't get thoughts of malice and sexual sadism out of his head. Though that was undoubtedly true, Sylvie didn't believe that to be the reason for his surprising return. He'd never before acknowledged his sickness when not institutionalized. Perhaps it was the heated racial tension of the general public at the time, or maybe it was the three square meals a day he'd become accustomed to during his stay. Either way, the doctors found out how true his statements were on the night of August 6th, 2003, when he managed to barricade himself and a young female intern in his room while the on-duty orderlies did everything they could to bust in. It didn't take them long to muscle their way through the door and that of the makeshift blockade that consisted of a heavy writing desk and a steel-framed bed, but it was long enough.

By the time the two men gained entry, Roger had severely beaten the poor young woman until she was unconscious on the floor. He had already pulled her pants down around her ankles, and he was untying the drawstrings of his scrub pants. Thankfully, that was as far as he had gotten before the first orderly through the door slammed Roger against the wall, restraining him from furthering his assault, while the other tended to the injured woman.

After those disturbing events, it was determined that the relaxed atmosphere and even more relaxed security measures of the Teton Psychiatric Hospital were not an adequate fit for someone with Roger's violent tendencies. A judge ruled he be remanded into the State's custody, but that he be transferred to the Somerset Psychiatric Institution for the Criminally Insane, a facility more capable of handling someone of Roger Loomis' regrettably explosive behavior.

And so, there he had remained, a patient for twenty years under the watchful eye of the hospital's medical staff, including Dr. Sylvie Zcieveteveicz's care over the past year and a half of those twenty.

He sat across from her, the two large psychiatric attendants looming heavily behind him, ready to spring into action should he act unfavorably during their session. It hadn't happened before, but they were under strict orders.

Sylvie offered Roger a kindly smile, as she always had, then opened her notebook to review the previous session's observations.

"Hello, Roger," she greeted, looking up from the opened pad on her lap. "How are you doing this morning?"

Roger curled his upper lip and grunted before licking his lower lip and squeezing his tongue between his teeth to keep from saying something he'd regret; something he'd learned from his last visit with the good doctor when she asked that he be taken away, due to his vulgar conduct. Sylvie took that as a sign that perhaps he wanted to open up about something.

"Is there something on your mind you'd like to discuss?" she asked.

"Why do we continue to meet out here instead of in your office?" Roger questioned, looking around the room to see who might be nearby before returning his stare in her direction. "Is it because you fear me?"

"Would it please you to learn I do?" Sylvie responded.

"No," Roger replied. "I've told you before; you have nothing to fear from me."

"Others would argue that fact, Roger. But, if what you say is true, you'll be happy to know it has nothing to do with you. But we aren't here to discuss *my* behavior, are we? This is *your* time, Roger. Why don't you tell me what's on your mind."

"You're the doctor with the secretive notes; why don't *you* tell me what's on my mind?"

Sylvie pressed her lips together and breathed in through her nose, faking the smile she'd maintained since the man sat down.

"Well," she said, glancing down at the open page of her notebook, "if you recall during our last meeting, you were telling me about that day at Teton - the day of the incident with a staff member. Would you like to continue from there?"

"There was no incident," he snorted. "I did as I was told."

"Yes, that's right," Sylvie responded. "I have it here in my notes. You claimed you were instructed to hurt that innocent girl, but you couldn't tell anyone who ordered you to do it or why. Is that correct?"

"So, you were listening after all," Roger said.

"I always listen to my patients."

"Do you?" Roger sneered, tilting his head sideways like a confused puppy. "And yet, after over a year, you still have no idea when I'm lying or speaking the truth."

"I'd like to think I have a pretty good idea," Sylvie replied. "But I'm not here to pass judgment. My job is to make you feel comfortable and to find out why you feel you need to lie at all. You're safe with me, Roger; you don't have to be afraid to share."

"You think I'm afraid?"

"Aren't you? Why else would you make up such a ridiculous story? Is it because you are afraid to admit the truth - that you have certain urges you have difficulty controlling?"

"Is that what you think?"

"We all have urges, Roger; there's nothing wrong with that. How we deal with them is what makes us who we are."

"If that's your professional analysis, doctor," Roger responded, "then I've misjudged you. I was wrong about you listening."

"Then make me listen, Roger," Sylvie appealed. "Tell me the truth about what happened that day."

"I've told you everything you need to hear, doctor. You have only to put the pieces together."

"I see. So then, if I am to believe you were instructed to do those awful things to that young intern, why not tell the judge at your trial? If it was determined you had been coerced, the judge may have shown leniency."

Roger looked down at his clasped hands in front of his crotch, his fingers intertwined so tightly that he was cutting the flow of circulation from the tips. Without raising his head, he shifted his eyes upward to look at her through his eyebrows.

"I was twenty-seven years old, in a mental hospital, and no way to prove my innocence that didn't make me look desperate. What would you have done? Nobody was going to believe a habitual sex offender. I was taking the fall, no matter what. And I knew where I'd be headed, so I figured, why not? There were worse places I could end up."

"If I'm not mistaken, you checked *yourself* into Teton, Roger; you could have filled out the appropriate paperwork and left there at any time - before you . . . did what you did."

"Do you think the doctors would have approved my release? You know my history, doctor, how I like the flesh of the young ones. Even they knew it would only have been a matter of time before I was back inside, only *not* of my will. Besides, if it was always going to be my eventual fate to be locked up here, in grand ol' Somerset, why not get a taste of that pretty young thing when I had the chance?"

He began to flap his tongue up and down disgustingly, causing the attendant behind him on his left to place a hand on his shoulder. At the subtle reminder, Roger ceased his behavior, turning his glance at the attendant's hand before smiling and quickly licking it, which prompted its hasty removal. He let out a distasteful snicker before turning back to Sylvie, where he dropped the mischievous façade for a more serious expression. Sylvie's visage remained unshaken by the man's disturbing glare.

"As I said, doctor," Roger continued, "you have nothing to fear from me; you're a little too old for my tastes." Then he shifted his stare behind her and pointed toward the large glass window over-looking the front courtyard, "But *that* one will do."

Surprised by his comment, Sylvie twisted in her chair to look where her troubled patient was pointing, only to be more shocked by what, or rather who, she saw.

Standing by the front window was Kevin Messier. He was peering in through the reinforced plate glass window with his hands above his eyebrows sandwiched between his forehead and the large pane to block the reflection from the sun. Once he saw Sylvie glance over at him, he peeled himself away from the glass and waved.

"I bet *he'd* be a fun one to play with," Sylvie heard Roger remark from over her shoulder.

Sylvie immediately spun around and shot Roger a detestable glare. "You're disgusting!" she yelled, letting her emotions sway her normally calm demeanor.

"There she is," Roger stated, a devious smirk penetrating his lips. "Glad to see *your* urges finally emerging."

"Take Mr. Loomis back to his room," she said through clenched teeth, her eyes shifting back and forth between the two attendants. "Get him out of my sight."

Without hesitation, the two burly staff members grabbed Roger by each arm and aggressively hoisted him from his chair. If Sylvie didn't know better, she would have thought they were looking for a reason to get physically rough with him. She wasn't complaining.

As they escorted Roger away, he shouted over his shoulder, "You think I don't know your secret, doctor?"

My secret? she thought, a distressed look on her face, doubting he meant anything by it. It was just one last jibe to rile her before he was out of view.

With the patient removed from the general assembly area, Sylvie turned her annoyed stare back to the young boy looking in through the window. Trying not to show her aggravation, she gestured to the boy's left, signaling for him to meet her at the front entrance. The boy was on state property at a psychiatric facility; he had no reason to be there. She didn't know how Kevin had gotten there or why he was poking around the building, but she was determined to find out what was going on.

Chapter 4

The Friends We Keep

The automatic sliding doors from the interior hallway opened into a small vestibule near the front entrance. A few chairs and a small table with outdated magazines on its surface decorated the otherwise empty entryway. To Sylvie's left, behind a small window of plexiglass, was Jules, the hospital's on-duty front desk attendant. She was the perfect person for the job with her jubilant, peppy attitude and perpetual smile. Across from Jules' visitor check-in station, along the right wall, was another plexiglass window into the Security Guard's office.

With a quick peek through the glass, Sylvie noticed the guard was not at his post.

"He's out front, sweetie," Jules chimed through the small opening at the base of her secured window. "Got himself a Peeping Tom."

"Thanks, Jules," Sylvie replied, peering out the front doors to find Glen (or "Guard Dog Glen" as the nurses called him) gripping Kevin's upper arm in one hand while his other reached for the radio strapped to his upper chest. Sylvie hastened her pace as the exterior sliding doors opened.

"It's all right, Glen," Sylvie stated excitedly, "he's with me."

"What's he doing wandering the grounds, Sylvie? I was just about to radio it in."

"Yeah, sorry. Before I noticed, he'd slipped away from me. You know kids; they're always curious."

"Yeah, well, his curiosity almost got him detained for a few hours," Glen said gruffly, looking down at the boy to put a scare into him.

"Yes, well, I'm sure he's learned his lesson; isn't that right, Kevin?" She squinted her eyes in disapproval.

The boy vigorously nodded his response.

"You need to keep a better eye on your visitors, Sylvie," the guard said, releasing his grip on the boy and nudging him toward the doctor.

"Thank you, Glen," she responded. "I'll make sure he doesn't leave my side."

As she turned back to head inside with Kevin in tow, Glen bellowed, "Hold it!"

They both froze in their tracks as if they'd suddenly been caught with their hands in the proverbial cookie jar.

"I still have to check the boy," the guard said, approaching from behind.

"Of course," Sylvie replied, faking a smile and relaxing her tense shoulders.

"Empty your front pockets," Glen ordered sternly as he quickly patted the boy's backside, then slid his hands down the pant legs to Kevin's sneakers. As Glen stood back up, Kevin pulled the linings of his front pockets out, dropping tightly wadded balls of lint onto the concrete below.

"All right; you're good to go."

Sylvie nodded at the guard.

"Thanks again, Glen," she said, placing her hand on Kevin's shoulder and gently tugging him forward while he fiddled with getting his pocket linings back in order.

"Just make sure he gets a visitor's badge and keeps it visible," Glen barked.

"Of course," she replied.

As they entered through the first set of sliding doors, leaving the "Guard Dog" behind to pick up the scraps of lint on the walkway, Sylvie rolled her eyes at Jules and gestured toward the interior doors, expressing her wish to have the young attendant buzz them in.

"Nice save, Sylvie," Jules uttered, sliding a visitor's badge on a lanyard through the small opening in the plexiglass.

"Don't get me started," Sylvie replied, swiping the badge from the window and shaking her head in mild frustration.

Jules smiled and winked, then pressed the button to admit their entrance.

Stepping through the door and taking a sharp left into the main hallway toward the stairs to the lower floor, Sylvie grasped Kevin's wrist, pulling him along. As much as she was annoyed at the boy's unexpected and inappropriate appearance, his sudden arrival caused her concern.

"What are you doing here, Kevin," she spoke in a hushed tone, handing him the badge. "You're really not supposed to be on the property unless you have business here."

"Seriously?" he replied. "I've snuck onto property way more secure than this."

"Do I even want to know?"

"It's probably better if you didn't ask."

Sylvie released his wrist as they entered the stairwell, keeping him by her side as they descended the dimly lit staircase to the even dimmer lower floor.

"How did you get here, anyway?" she asked.

"It's only a few miles from my house; I rode my bike. I stashed it down the street behind the dumpster at O'Leary's Diner."

Kevin slowed his pace as they neared the bottom of the stairs, something Sylvie discerned immediately.

"What's wrong?" she asked, noticing the boy's nervous stare as he peered down the hallway, where the only light seemed to be coming from a flickering fluorescent bulb along the ceiling in the distance.

"Did we take a wrong turn or something?"

"No, my office is right down the hall."

"Down here?" Kevin questioned. "This is like the land maintenance forgot or something."

"Tell me about it," Sylvie responded. "I don't like coming down here alone. Come on." She nodded her head sideways, urging the boy onward. "You can protect me if anything jumps out at us."

She smirked, taking a step backward into the darkened hallway. Kevin grinned nervously.

"I'm joking, Kevin; come on."

Sylvie turned and started for her office, digging into her pants pocket to retrieve her keys. Kevin scuffled along after her, his eyes scanning ahead to gauge the distance to what he hoped was her door fast approaching on the right. It was.

Unlocking the door and flicking the light switch on the wall, Sylvie hadn't the chance to get out of the way before the anxious boy quickly squeezed by her to step into the lighted office.

"Sure, come on in," she said playfully, holding back a slight giggle as she closed the door behind her. "Have a seat," she continued, pointing to the wheeled office chair at the front of her desk as she tossed her keys onto a stack of folders by her keyboard. As the boy sat down, she slid herself to the front of the desk and leaned her butt against the edge, her arms folded about her chest with her legs crossed at the ankles.

"So, are you going to answer my question from earlier?" she asked. "Why are you here, Kevin? What's going on?"

"You said if I ever needed to talk . . ."

"Yes, that's true. But I meant outside of my work, sweetie. You're not supposed to be here. Some of the patients can get triggered by certain things. Seeing a boy sneaking around outside could make them feel a little uneasy. And not meaning to scare you, but some could even be dangerous."

"What about that guy you were talking to? Is *he* dangerous?"

"Oh, Mr. Loomis . . ? He . . . ," Sylvie paused, glancing sideways and slightly nodding her head before continuing, "has the potential to be violent, yes. But we aren't here to discuss my patients; this is about you. So, talk to me."

"I just don't like being home, that's all."

"Okay. Would you care to tell me why?"

The boy's leg began bouncing nervously. He leaned forward in his chair and stared down at his shoes to avoid making eye contact with Sylvie.

"You can tell me anything, Kevin. It stays between us. I promise" She unfolded her arms and drew an X across her chest with her index finger. It felt like something she was supposed to do, even though the boy hadn't noticed since he still had his eyes averted.

"It's just that . . ." He slowly rolled his eyes upward to catch Sylvie staring down at him, a sympathetic look on her face.

"Yes?"

"My parents fight a lot. They're always yelling at each other. I can't stand to hear it, so I have to get out of there."

"Oh, honey, I'm sorry to hear that." She leaned forward and placed her hand on his shoulder.

"I think they're going to get divorced," he continued. "My friend Bradley told me when his parents started arguing all the time, they got divorced five months later."

"I'm sorry to say," Sylvie returned, "that does happen sometimes. But that doesn't mean yours are going to. Sometimes people need time to work out their differences, but until they do, they disagree on things."

"But I feel like it's my fault," Kevin said, his voice cracking. "Like I keep doing something wrong to make them argue like they do."

"No, Kevin, you can't think like that. Adults can be stubborn and, at times, a little selfish. Sometimes it's difficult for married couples to communicate how they feel. And when that happens, it's harder for either of them to compromise. They forget that there's someone else who is also affected. But it has nothing to do with you. I'm sure of it. So, you need to stop blaming yourself."

"Did your parents divorce, Sylvie?"

Sylvie's eyes widened from Kevin's surprising question, and the room became silent as she quickly tried to gather her thoughts.

"Oh, um . . ," she stumbled for the words, "well, that um . . . I mean, no, my parents didn't get divorced." She shrugged her shoulders and offered a forced sideways smirk.

"Really? So they're still married?"

Sylvie's response never came as the lights suddenly flickered, causing them both to look up at the ceiling fixture.

"What was that?" Kevin questioned.

"That was a sign, kiddo," she replied, pushing herself from the desk and snatching her keys from atop the folder they sat on. "I think someone wants me to get back to work. And you've got to be going. Come on; let's get you back upstairs."

"Is there a way we can skip the creepy hallway?" Kevin joked as Sylvie opened the door.

"Believe me; if there was a way . . ."

She stood with the door open as Kevin reluctantly stepped by her into the hallway. He took a couple of steps toward the staircase and then froze. As Sylvie locked the office door, she noticed how stiff the boy had become.

"Oh, it's not that bad, Kevin; stop exaggerating."

"It's not that, Sylvie," he responded. "Can't you hear it? Something's going on?"

"What are you talking about; I don't hear . . ."
Her words were cut short by the sudden sound of

hurried footsteps stamping down the staircase ahead of them. She grabbed Kevin's shoulder and pulled him back toward her as if suspecting someone dangerous to turn the corner in front of them. Seconds later, her grip on the boy's shoulder loosened, and her muscles relaxed as the surgeon, Dr. Lee, rounded the corner.

"Thank goodness you're down here, Sylvie," the doctor expressed in a panic. "There's been an incident."

"What is it, Dr. Lee? What's happened?"

"Roger broke away from the orderlies and is threatening Greta." The doctor shifted his eyes to Kevin and then back to Sylvie. "He's asking for you."

Chapter 5

Urgency

"Shit!"

She quickly looked at Kevin and gave him an apologetic glance. "Sorry for the language, Kevin. There's a situation I have to deal with. Let's get you out of here, shall we?"

Kevin nodded his approval, his eyes wide with fear. Sylvie walked alongside the boy, pressing her palm against the back of his shoulder to pull him along. She hoped it would also relieve his nervousness.

They rushed up the stairs with Dr. Lee leading the way. As they approached the main entrance, Sylvie stepped in front of Kevin and turned to face him to halt his advancement.

"This is where we part ways, kiddo. Dr. Lee will make sure you make it out safe and sound."

She glanced at the surgeon and nodded.

"Certainly," was the doctor's reply.

"Take it easy, Kevin, and remember what I said."

"I will, Sylvie," he answered, nodding.

"Okay, now go." She removed her hand from his shoulder and nodded sideways toward the sliding doors.

"This way, Kevin," Dr. Lee jumped in as Sylvie turned her attention in the opposite direction toward the Day Room.

Shaking her head and hurrying her pace, she hoped she wasn't too late. She wondered what could have gotten into Roger to cause him to suddenly act out in such a manner (as if the unstable man's tendency toward violent behavior somehow needed explanation).

She scanned her badge at the first locked door, listening for the familiar click of the latch as it unlocked, giving her access to the other doctors' offices along "Doctors' Row" to her left, with the nurses' station and staff break room directly across from the doctors' offices. Straight ahead of her, along the right wall, were two single-stall employee bathrooms, and across from them, an elevator leading to the business and executive offices on the second floor. In front of her, beyond the elevator and the bathrooms, was a second door of reinforced glass, one of two entrances into the facility's Day Room, the activities hall for the patients.

Unlocking the door with her badge, she entered to find Dr. Prichard and "Guard Dog" Glen standing in the middle of the floor, their backs to her as they tried to gain control over the rapidly deteriorating situation. And that situation was Roger Loomis.

He was standing behind Greta Lambeau with one arm wrapped around her upper chest, squeezing her tightly to him, his other hand threatening to jab a pointed plastic object into her neck. Most of the other patients had already been escorted from the large gathering room shortly after the incident began. The few that remained were timidly huddled at the back of a sofa behind Roger, cut off from the rescuing hands of the hospital's staff.

"You don't come near me!" Roger shouted, his head shifting back and forth between the guard and Dr. Prichard. "I told you, I want to talk to the other one, Dr. Shit-a-bitch."

"It's Zcieveteveicz," Sylvie's voice rang out, "and I'm right here, Roger."

Glen and Dr. Prichard turned in her direction as Roger leaned sideways to catch sight of Sylvie approaching from behind the older doctor, who was blocking his view.

"You don't want to do this, Roger," Sylvie continued, keeping composed as she stepped beside her co-worker. "Put the weapon down, and let's talk this out. You have nothing to gain by hurting Miss Lambeau."

"I have nothing to lose either. We both know I'll be in here until I'm dead."

"You do have something to lose, Roger," she responded. "You'd lose my respect."

Dr. Prichard twisted in place and shot Sylvie a disapproving glance, of which she took immediate notice.

"And the respect of Dr. Prichard, as well," she added to appease the older doctor.

"I don't give a shit about Dr. Prick-ard," Roger bellowed, pulling the plastic object from Greta's neck to point it at the tenured doctor, allowing Sylvie to see it was the handle of a plastic spoon that had broken, leaving a pointed end. It wasn't the most dangerous of weapons, but sharp enough to pierce the older woman's skin should Roger not listen to reason. He pressed the spoon handle back to Greta's neck as he seethed.

"Why is he even here?" Roger questioned, squeezing his captive tighter. "I want him to leave. I want them all to go."

"I'll tell you what, Roger," Sylvie responded, "if Dr. Prichard leaves, will you let Miss Lambeau go?"

The older doctor's stare stabbed knives into Sylvie before she had even finished her counter.

"Now, hold on!" Dr. Prichard argued. "I don't think . . ."

"I don't give a fuck what you think, doc," Roger yelled, the quiet moans of Greta sounding out as the point of the plastic handle pressed harder against her neck. "I'm talking to the lady."

Sylvie turned to her colleague and flashed her eyes sideways toward the door. "It's all right, Doctor; I've got this."

Dr. Prichard exhaled heavily through his nose, his disapproval conveyed, and his daggered stare meeting with equal resistance. He shook his head and sneered.

"I'll go, but if something goes wrong, this is on you."

Sylvie nodded. "I know."

He gave a final angry glance toward Roger before conceding and walking away. Sylvie watched until the door closed behind him before she turned back to her agitated patient.

"You see now, Roger? Dr. Prichard is gone as you wanted. I believe it's your turn to do as I requested. Please release Miss Lambeau."

"I want the guard and orderlies gone too," Roger demanded, spit spraying from his mouth.

Sylvie looked at him sternly and shook her head. "That's not gonna happen."

"I ain't going anywhere, Loomis," Glen spoke.

"That goes double for me," Tremont added, stepping forward from behind another attendant. "I ain't letting you alone with Miss Z."

"Well," Sylvie said, shrugging her shoulders, "it would seem we've reached an impasse. What's it going to be, Roger? Don't make this more difficult than it needs to be."

"What's it going to be?" he yelled. "What's it going to be? I'll tell you exactly what it's going to be. This old bitch needs to die." He gritted his teeth and pressed the broken plastic harder into Greta's neck. She let out a labored gasp. "That's right; she's going to . . ."

Before he could finish his sentence, he felt the concussive force of a hard wooden cane slam against the back of his head, jolting him forward and causing him to release Greta. It happened so quickly that Greta herself hadn't even the time to crumple to the ground before Glen and two psych attendants charged forward to restrain the momentarily dazed man.

Roger refrained from struggling as his subduers hastily removed him from the room. Sylvie quickly went to Greta's side to check on her while the remaining nurses and attendants stepped in to calm the other startled patients. Lightly holding onto Greta's arm, Sylvie took a moment to glance up and offer an approving nod to the woman's unexpected savior. It was Mrs. Landry, an unusual woman, even for one in a psych ward. But Sylvie's thoughts wouldn't stay with the woman as her attention veered toward the door.

What the hell was that all about, she thought, pondering the man's unexpected actions? *What was it that set Roger off?*

Chapter 6

Second Thoughts

Sylvie knew she was in for an earful before she set foot in Dr. Prichard's office. The man was a pompous ass who couldn't stand the thought of being shown up by a younger doctor, let alone a female one. She knew there was no way around this inevitable outcome the moment she sent him away. And as she walked through the open door of his office, where he and Dr. Lee were discussing his dissatisfaction with the unsettling events, the room became silent. Dr. Prichard was sitting behind his desk, looking perturbed, while Dr. Lee stood silently in front of it, his guilt-ridden expression telling Sylvie everything she needed to know. His uncomfortable glance was a subtle indication of things to come. Dr. Prichard had more in store.

"You mind telling me what that was all about in there?" he questioned, his squinted stare burning a hole through her. "That man was threatening to kill that woman, and you catered to his demands like that?"

"That man and woman have names, Doctor," she replied.

"Don't give me any of your sympathetic bullshit; I know they have names. I know both of them better than you ever will. I want to know why you thought it would be a good idea to let a maniac like Roger Loomis control the situation out there."

"Do you make a habit of calling your patients maniacs?" Sylvie questioned, her eyes narrow.

"Don't get smart with me, Missy; you know what I meant."

"With all due respect, Doctor, *I* was the one that had the situation under control."

"The hell you did!"

"Maybe I should step out," Dr. Lee timidly stated, dropping his eyes to the floor.

"No, you stay put," Dr. Prichard demanded. "I want you to hear first-hand how incapable Dr. Zcieveteveicz is in her chosen field."

"Excuse me?" Sylvie questioned, agitated.

"You heard me, Doctor. We're not running a goddamn circus here. We can't let the patients take advantage of our goodwill like that. Your little stunt out there has probably set some of the other patients' recovery back years. That woman . . ,"

"Greta," Sylvie sternly interrupted.

"That woman," the older doctor continued, ignoring Sylvie, "will be traumatized for months."

"First of all," Sylvie jumped in, having heard enough, "Greta will be fine. She's stronger than you give her credit for. Secondly, Roger was demanding to talk with *me*, not you. Your continuing efforts to try to talk him down, and talk down *to* him, could have triggered him further and caused him to harm Greta."

"And you think giving in to him and asking me to walk away was a better idea?" Dr. Prichard argued.

"The situation was controlled, wasn't it?" she answered. "Greta is now safe."

"You made us look divided."

"It demonstrated that we're willing to listen," Sylvie snapped back. "That's all most of these people want; to know that someone is listening to them – listening to their stories."

"Of course, I'm listening; it's my job, for Christ's sake," the older doctor flared.

"I don't mean just hearing what they're telling you. I mean, *really* listening to them."

"What kind of horseshit are you spewing? Do you think I don't know my job? Well, let me tell you something, sweetheart; I've been doing this for a long time - since you were in diapers. I'm a tenured doctor at this facility; I know what these patients need and how to keep them in check."

"Are you even listening to yourself?" Sylvie questioned. "You've got your head stuck so far up your ass, you're unable to hear anything but the sound of your own flatulence."

"What did you say to me?" Dr. Prichard fumed, sitting forward in his chair.

"You've just proven my point, Doctor," Sylvie said, smirking. "You're not even listening to *me*, and I'm right in front of you."

Without waiting for a response, Sylvie turned and walked out of the office, frustrated by the arrogance of the older doctor. She heard some shuffling behind her before a voice rang out.

"Sylvie, hold up."

Dr. Lee had found himself following her lead, walking out of Dr. Prichard's office. Sylvie continued her stride, listening to the hurried footsteps of her colleague as he tried to catch up with her. When she reached the end of the hallway, she stopped and turned, granting him a reprieve from his rushed pace.

"That man infuriates me sometimes," she stated, her teeth clenched. "I'll give *him* 'sweetheart,' the self-righteous jackass. And to think, I went in there to apologize."

"I know, I know," Dr. Lee responded, placing his hand on Sylvie's lower back to coerce her around the corner in case Dr. Prichard should leave his office and see the two of them together. "I understand your frustration, but you can't let him get to you like that."

"Easy for you to say; he *likes* you. Or, at least, he doesn't feel threatened by you."

"I don't think that's it, Sylvie. Prichard knows you're a good psychologist. He's just been under a lot of stress lately with what's been going on."

"What do you mean? What's been going on?" she asked, suddenly showing concern.

"Have you heard of what's been happening over in Southbridge?"

"The murders?" Sylvie questioned.

"That's right," Dr. Lee confirmed. "There's some kind of serial killer or something, cutting letters into people."

"Yeah, I've seen the news. They're calling him The Alphabet Killer. What's that got to do with . . ,"

"Dr. Prichard's daughter and grandkids live in Southbridge."

"Oh, shit!" Sylvie let slip, immediately covering her mouth with her hand.

"Yeah, it's scary to think about."

"Wow; now I feel bad for thinking what I did about him."

"Well, don't feel *too* bad," Dr. Lee said, placing his hand on her shoulder. "The man is still a pompous ass. I just thought you should know that it's not *all* personal."

Sylvie nodded, "Thank you, Dr. Lee."

"No problem," he replied. Then, after giving a nod and a smile, he started toward his office. "For what it's worth, Sylvie," the doctor stated, glancing over his shoulder while he continued forward, "I think you did the right thing in there."

Sylvie smiled as she leaned her back against the wall. Bringing her hand to her forehead and closing her eyes, she thought of Dr. Lee's last words.

I think you did the right thing in there.

She snickered to herself and shook her head, then took a deep breath and opened her eyes. She glanced back down the hall, but Dr. Lee had already vanished into his office. And although he was no longer present, his words still resonated with her.

I think you did the right thing in there.

She believed it too. It's why she did what she did. Still, she wondered why doing the right thing always seemed to bite her in the ass. If not with her colleagues, then with her patients.

Not this time, she thought. *I won't let that happen.* She pushed herself from the wall with renewed confidence and headed toward the Day Room.

She knew the rest of the staff believed her methods to be a bit unusual. She didn't care. Trust was an earned thing, especially for those with mental health disorders. Gaining the patients' confidence was essential in the process; it was what she needed to do. No matter what the others thought, she wouldn't let her unorthodox methods backfire on her. She couldn't. Dr. Prichard's personal feelings aside, there was a reason she came to this hospital, and she'd be damned if she was going to let that arrogant asshole deter her from doing what she needed to do.

Dr. Lee's words rang out again.

I think you did the right thing in there.

And as she took her place in the familiar chair to wait for her next patient, she thought to herself.

It's okay, Sylvie. Get yourself together. You've got a job to do. You're here for a reason. You can make this work. You can still make things right.

Chapter 7

The Odd Mrs. Landry

The woman sitting in the wheelchair across from her looked timid and unassuming. She wasn't someone you'd expect would put up a fight against an angry aggressor, let alone act violently *toward* said aggressor. Even so, there she sat, Mrs. Landry, hero of the hospital - so nicknamed by her fellow ward mates after having saved Greta from possible injury or death. It wasn't a horrible moniker, and certainly better than her previously held title, "The Odd Mrs. Landry."

Sylvie never approved of that name, especially when one of her co-workers would let it slip. She could forgive the other patients since they were the woman's peers, and some of them didn't always have the capacity for self-control, but the staff knew better, and yet, she would still catch them slinging the offensive banter.

The older woman *was* strange, of that, there was no doubt. And although the same was true about most of the patients at Somerset, Mrs. Landry was a step above. She'd never been married yet insisted on being referred to as *Mrs.* Landry. When asked why it was so important to her, she responded that she took the title from her mother. When asked about its significance, she stated it was a reminder that there were evil people in the world, though she couldn't remember why she thought that. It wasn't dementia or the onset of Alzheimer's; during their numerous sessions, the woman demonstrated that she fully maintained her faculties. She was just, well, "odd," and the matching moniker soon followed.

It was more the way she carried herself and spoke of things as if she knew more than what she was supposed to know. When asked how she could know such things, her response was always the same: "Never you mind," like she was holding onto some grand secret.

She also had a way with her words – a particular way she would phrase things - like new age lingo she would constantly get wrong. Sometimes, it was funny, even if she didn't think so herself. It certainly made for some amusing discussions, something Sylvie hoped would be the case during their current meeting, but she knew that was too much to expect given the seriousness of the subject matter.

"So, how are you today, Mrs. Landry?"

"How should I be?" the woman replied.

"Well, there was a lot of excitement today," Sylvie responded. "Wouldn't you agree?"

"The stuff with that clown, Loomis?"

"That's right. It was quite the thing you did in there."

"It was nothing," Mrs. Landry said, flopping her hand to dismiss the statement while looking away.

"I disagree, Mrs. Landry. And I think Greta would as well; you may have saved her life."

The older woman perked up, "Oh yeah, that Greta, she's my jelly."

"I think you mean jam."

"Why would I mean jam?"

"It's just an expression," Sylvie stated, a slight smile breaching her lips.

"It's a *stupid* expression. But, at least it's not shitty marmalade."

"Okay, we'll go with that, then." Sylvie dipped her head down to prevent herself from laughing out loud. She didn't want Mrs. Landry taking offense. Once she gathered herself, she cleared her throat and looked back at the aged woman.

"If you don't mind, I'd like to discuss what happened."

"What's there to talk about?"

"Well, I wanted to make sure you were doing okay. To witness someone being threatened, especially a friend, can be a rather traumatic experience."

"Traumatic experience? Being threatened? By that bozo?"

"You don't think what happened here earlier was frightening?"

"Why would I? It was all an act."

"An act?" Sylvie questioned. "Mrs. Landry, why would you say such a thing?"

Mrs. Landry silently stared into Sylvie's eyes for a moment before answering, "Never you mind."

"All right then," Sylvie responded, jotting a note onto the open page of her pad. "Still, if it was only an act, it was quite convincing. He had *me* fooled."

"You can't kid a kidder," the old woman mumbled, "but you can almost always fool a fool."

"What was that?" Sylvie questioned, thinking she must have misheard the woman.

"Never you mind."

Discouraged, Sylvie exhaled loudly and sat back in her chair, draping her arms across the pad on her lap. After a few silent seconds, she continued.

"Mrs. Landry – act or not, I'd like to talk about Mr. Loomis' actions today. He could have seriously injured himself or someone else."

"Not Greta," Mrs. Landry announced sharply, sitting forward in her chair. "She's too tough."

"She *is* tough," Sylvie agreed, nodding her head. "Perhaps tougher than Mr. Loomis counted on. As are you. That was a brave thing you did, helping your friend like that. I should tell you, however, that although everything worked out for the best, it was also dangerous. You can't act out like that, Mrs. Landry. It could have jeopardized everyone's safety, including yours. Do you understand?"

"Yeah, yeah," the woman replied.

"Okay, good. Now that that's out of the way, let's talk for a moment about what happened. You seemed to have been right there in the thick of it. I'm curious to learn if you had seen or heard something that might have caused Roger to act out in such a way?"

"You mean if it wasn't all just for show?" Mrs. Landry reminded the doctor.

"Right, if it wasn't all just for show."

"Oh, I'd probably tell you it wasn't anything from today. Roger didn't like Greta very much after what she had done all those years back. He probably felt he needed retribution. He probably wanted her to suffer when he found out the truth. That's what I'd probably tell you. You know, if any of that had been real."

"Oh, so something happened between those two in the past?"

"I've already said too much," Mrs. Landry stated, shifting her head from side to side as if suspicious of someone else listening.

"But if it was all in pretense," Sylvie suggested, "I'm sure it wouldn't matter if . . ,"

"Never you mind! Never you mind!" the woman began to shout, startling Sylvie and gaining the attention of the two psychiatric attendants across the large room.

"I'm sorry for upsetting you, Mrs. Landry," Sylvie apologized. "We don't have to talk about that anymore."

The usually calm and unassuming woman abruptly stood from her wheelchair, pointing her finger at Sylvie. "Never you mind! Never you mind! Never you mind!"

Sylvie slid her chair backward several inches, surprised and unprepared for the older woman's sudden boisterous actions. She made no effort to stop Mrs. Landry's ranting as she noticed one of the attendants approaching from behind the woman. As he placed his hand on the excited woman's shoulder, her yelling ceased.

"I ain't done nothing wrong," Mrs. Landry remarked, staring down the doctor with squinted eyes.

"Of course not," Sylvie responded.

"Then, you can call off your watchdog."

"Mrs. Landry, I assure you, Samuel is only here for your safety." She nodded at the young man.

"My safety, huh?"

"That's right. You got a little excited there, jumping from your chair. Not to mention, you looked a little unsteady without your cane. We wouldn't want you falling over. This gentleman is here to help you back into your seat."

"What if I don't want to sit anymore?"

"Well, that *is* your choice," Sylvie replied, "but after the recent spills you've had, I'd feel more comfortable if you remained in your chair. Plus, I would like it if you sat back down so we could continue our discussion. Do you think we could do that?"

"Nothing more about Greta or Loomis," the old woman demanded, pointing her finger at the doctor.

"That's fine," Sylvie agreed, nodding. "Not another word."

Mrs. Landry continued to stare at Sylvie, reading her facial expression. When she deemed the words sincere, the woman responded.

"I'll sit."

She looked over her shoulder and sneered at the attendant whose hand was still on her. She then shrugged forward in defiance, expressing her dissatisfaction with being touched. Sylvie glanced at the man and nodded, who removed his hand from the patient's shoulder.

"Hmph! You're lucky I don't hit *you* with my cane," she said, glaring at the man.

The attendant smirked.

Mrs. Landry reached down and grabbed the armrests of her wheelchair, her own arms straining to support her weight as she plopped herself down.

"Now that wasn't so bad, was it?" Sylvie began with a smile. She glanced up at the attendant, "Thank you, Samuel. I think I've got it from here." Samuel nodded and smiled. "No problem, Doctor."

"Well, now I feel better," Sylvie said, shifting her attention back to the woman. "And I hope you do as well, Mrs. Landry."

The older woman threw her hands forward in disgust as the attendant backed away.

"Never you mind."

"Right," Sylvie acquiesced. "So then, may we talk about why you think you don't belong here with us?"

"Why do you think that?"

"It's my job to listen to people, Mrs. Landry. You've expressed your feelings on numerous occasions about how you don't belong here, even though we've done everything we can to make things comfortable for you. So, if you truly believe that, tell me, why don't you feel you belong here?"

"I may have felt that way before," Mrs. Landry said, "but all that changed a little while back."

"Oh? And why is that?" Sylvie inquired. "What changed your mind?"

"Let's just say the personnel around here took a twist for the better."

Believing the words meant for her, Sylvie smiled, accepting the unspoken compliment.

"I think you mean, 'a turn for the better.'"

"Why would I mean that?"

Sylvie smirked, "No reason."

The women sat silently for a moment, each acknowledging the other's presence without the need for words. It was the first calm moment of the day, Sylvie thought. What a shame it had to come to an end. Especially with the subject she was about to broach.

"Mrs. Landry - I'd like to talk to you about your sister. May we do that?"

The "Hero of the Hospital" didn't say a word as she glared at the doctor through hollow eyes.

"Did you hear me, Mrs. Landry? I'd like to . . ,"

"I heard you," the woman bellowed. "I don't want to talk about her."

"But I think it's important we discuss what happened."

"You *know* what happened. We had gotten into an argument, and now we're no longer on speaking terms."

"I think there's a little more to it than that."

"You can think what you want, but there ain't."

"But Mrs. Landry . . ,"

"Never you mind!" she yelled. "I don't think I want to sit here anymore."

She grabbed at the wheels to back away but struggled to make the chair move, confused about how to unlock the brakes. After wrestling with it for a moment with little success, Sylvie raised her hand and waved one of the attendants forward.

"It's okay, Mrs. Landry," Sylvie assured the woman, "this kind gentleman will get you to where you're going."

"Hmph!" was all Mrs. Landry could squeak out as Samuel unlocked the wheels and wheeled her away.

As Sylvie watched Mrs. Landry being rolled from the activities hall, she couldn't help wondering if she was ever going to get that woman to crack. The session hadn't been as productive as she had hoped. It had been over a year, yet the woman continued to shut down as soon as the subject of her sister arose. Getting the woman to open up about what had happened between the two of them had become a major goal of Sylvie's. She had all the confidence she'd eventually break through - if given enough time. That was the unknown.

Will there be enough time, she thought, *before I . . .*

It was a thought that would wait for another time. For now, it was on to her next patient.

Chapter 8

Reclusive

She remembered the words Mrs. Landry spoke as Greta sat down.

It was all an act.

She thought it strange that the woman would say such a thing. Having been present during the experience, Sylvie knew it wasn't an act and thought maybe Greta could shed some light on her friend's comment. If not the comment, then perhaps that of what she understood about the attack on her.

"Hi, Greta," Sylvie began with her soothing voice. "I wanted to give you some time after what happened earlier today. Are you sure you're ready to speak with me?"

"Am I ever ready?"

"I'd like to think so."

"Why *are* we meeting anyway?" Greta asked. "This isn't our usual day."

"I understand that," Sylvie replied. "But after what happened, I thought it best if we met and discussed. Would that be all right with you?"

"You're the doctor," the woman responded. "Or have you forgotten that you reminded me of that fact the last time we met?"

"I haven't forgotten, no. I also told you we needed to be more productive in our sessions. I hope this can be that time."

"I'll make an effort."

"Great! Perhaps now we can talk about your feelings from today's earlier incident. That must have been quite a scary moment for you. Can you tell me what that was all about?"

"Why don't you ask Roger?" Greta answered. "I'm sure he'll be more than willing to answer you."

"I'll be meeting with Mr. Loomis as well, but I think it's important that I hear from both of you. This is your opportunity to share *your* side of the story."

"The man's an erratic buffoon," she shouted. "*That's* my side of the story."

"He *can* be erratic at times, yes. Did you notice anything that might have set him off? Was he provoked in any way?"

"What are you saying – that this is *my* fault? That I did something to upset him? I was the victim in all of that."

"I wasn't saying that at all," Sylvie replied. "I'm just trying to learn if there were any warning signs before his attack. It could help prevent another such outburst."

"Outburst, my ass! He tried to kill me. And if you professional mucky-mucks can't figure out that fucker, what makes you think we patients can?"

Sylvie displayed a disappointing look. "That was unnecessary, Greta," she said brusquely before continuing. "Had he ever threatened you before?"

Suddenly, Greta went silent and shifted her eyes downward to the right. Sylvie received her answer - if not verbally, then with Greta's silent reaction.

"So he *has* threatened you before," Sylvie stated.

"It's nothing."

"How can you say that, Greta? Nobody here should ever feel threatened."

"You think *that* dimwit asshole is threatening? Sweetheart, you haven't been here long enough to learn . . ," Greta silenced herself again.

"To learn what?" Sylvie questioned, shaking her head.

She waited for an answer, but the woman's lips remained tightly clasped while she stared blankly into the doctor's eyes. Sylvie let out a frustrated breath, then jotted some words into her notebook.

"So, you don't want to tell me?" Sylvie inquired, still writing notes about the patient. "I get it, Greta. I know it's sometimes difficult to trust others." She looked up from her pad at the older woman to show her sincerity. "But you can trust *me*. I'm here to listen if you need any help." Sylvie expected a response, but none came. "Okay, then," she continued, feeling slightly frustrated. "You know, that was quite a bold thing Mrs. Landry did, don't you agree? I mean, even though she thought the whole thing was an act."

"She said that?" Greta questioned, suddenly interested in what Sylvie had to say.

"She did. Why do you suppose she would say something like that?"

"I'll tell you why," Greta replied. "Because that woman has a big mouth and talks too much."

"Or maybe not enough."

Greta looked at Sylvie curiously.

"What do you mean?" the woman questioned, her eyes narrow.

"Oh, it's nothing, really. Just . . , Mrs. Landry mentioned something had happened between you and Roger some time ago - before I arrived here - but she wouldn't tell me what it was. Would you care to elaborate?"

"Let's just say," Greta began, the corner of her lip curled up, "that man is sick in the head and lies about everything. Watch yourself around him, girly; do you hear me? I can't be your goddamn babysitter."

"Greta, is that concern I hear in your voice?" Sylvie smiled. It was the first time the older woman had shown any semblance of an emotional connection with her.

"I'm just saying, is all," Greta blurted. "There's no need to get all sappy about it."

"Well, thank you anyway, Greta; I'll take your words into advisement. But, if you're unwilling to talk to me about the whole Roger situation, perhaps we can discuss the other topic you continually try to avoid."

"You mean my past?"

"You can't avoid it forever."

"The hell I can't. Do you think I want to remember that shit? It's what got me locked up in here."

"It is, indeed," Sylvie agreed, nodding. "But I also know it's difficult for you to accept the reason behind your sentence. Maybe we can work to resolve your confusion - or, at the very least, your frustration."

Greta sneered at the doctor. "Do you even know who I was?"

"I have to be honest," Sylvie answered, "I didn't when I first started working here. But after I read your file, I spent a weekend binge-watching a few of your movies. I have to say, Greta, you were quite talented."

"Damn right, I was," Greta muttered. "Then that bastard took it all away from me."

"Henry?"

"I don't speak of him," Greta stated, folding her arms about her chest and turning her head away.

"Can you make an exception? Just for today?"

"I don't think so."

"But Greta, I'd really like to learn about the man who . . ,"

"I said, 'I don't think so!'" the woman snapped. "Besides . . , nothing remains a secret for too long in this place. We have no privacy. Every little thing we do gets recorded in somebody's notebook, so quit pretending like you don't know things."

"Very well," Sylvie stated, hosting a forced smile. "We don't have to talk about him. Only when you're ready."

"You say that as if you think I'm ever going to tell you."

Sylvie looked at the older woman, straight-faced, before flashing a subtle grin that slowly transformed into a full-blown smile.

"You will; I'll warm up to you yet."

Sylvie tapped her hands on her knees and pushed herself up from the chair. "But I think we'll leave it at that for today. I want to thank you for meeting with me, Greta. And I'm so glad you are all right after this morning's excitement. I'll see you for our regular appointment."

Sylvie glanced across the room and waved to the nearest psychiatric attendant to help deliver the aged woman back to her room. Before the attendant arrived, Greta looked up at Sylvie's optimistic expression and sighed.

"You're going to see Loomis next, ain'tcha?" Greta questioned.

Sylvie tilted her head downward to give her attention to the woman.

"I am."

"Remember what I told you," Greta said. "Watch yourself. That man can't be trusted; he's dangerous."

"Thank you, Greta," Sylvie responded, smiling. "I'm not afraid of Mr. Loomis. I'll be fine."

The arriving attendant gently placed his hand on Greta's shoulder to signal his presence. "Come on now, Miss Lambeau; let's get you back to your room."

Greta rose from her chair and slapped his hand away.

"I'm old, not helpless," she snapped.

"No problem, ma'am," the attendant smiled. "I'll just keep you company while we walk."

With the attendant by her side, Greta turned and walked away. While they did, Sylvie thought of the woman's words.

Nothing remains a secret for too long in this place.

Sylvie hoped that wasn't true. Some secrets were safer kept locked away. But she couldn't worry about that at the moment. She glanced to her left to see Dr. Prichard standing by the doorway, glaring at her. She had felt his burning stare upon her since Greta first sat down but didn't dare look in his direction for fear it would distract her from her session with the older woman. Once he'd been alerted to her knowledge of his overbearing presence, the doctor glanced at his watch in an attempt to disguise his being there as something other than keeping an eye on her. It didn't sit well with Sylvie. She was aware of Dr. Prichard's disapproval of her methods, but the man could at least have the decency to tell her to her face instead of criticizing her from a distance.

He might be going through some personal shit, she thought, *but it doesn't give him the right to demean those of us around him.*

She watched him turn and step arrogantly through the doorway, his chin raised. As much as his cocky behavior infuriated her, it didn't matter. It wouldn't stop her from continuing on her path and doing what she needed to do, which, at the moment, was to talk with Roger Loomis.

But only for now.

Chapter 9

Sound Advice

Perhaps it was a mistake, her coming here, thinking she could make a difference. The patients weren't responding to her unique methods as she'd hoped they would. She only wanted them to feel comfortable and safe, in their own environment, amongst their peers, instead of being separated and alone in a claustrophobic office. Even in the open space of the large assembly area, she always made sure there was privacy so they could openly talk. Truthfully, it was for her own comfort and safety as well. Down on the lower floor where sound didn't travel well - if something were to happen . . , well, she didn't want to think about that. Especially not after what had happened that morning - and in a crowded room. For the patients at Somerset, with their sometimes erratic behavioral issues, anything was possible. And yet, there she stood, outside the door of the man responsible for the morning's excitement, and the reason for this unscheduled and secluded visit.

Whatever his intentions, Roger Loomis' actions only succeeded in getting him banished to his room for a week, sheltered inside with no interaction with the other patients, and under constant supervision by a staff member. It was this hospital's lighter version of solitary confinement. They had a harsher version too, but since nobody was injured during the incident, it was Dr. Prichard's recommendation Roger be kept secluded from the others in the comfort of his own room instead of a padded one. He thought it would teach the patient a lesson regarding his psychiatric outburst. The doctor's decision was unexpected. Although Sylvie agreed with the easier punishment, feeling the harsher alternative was more detrimental to a patient's recovery, it had never been Dr. Prichard's approach to take it easy on a patient.

Maybe the man was human, after all, she thought.

Sylvie stood beside Tremont, the attendant assigned watch duty, staring in through the door's small window to get a sense of Roger's temperament. He was seated at a small wooden desk along the far wall facing away from the door. His legs were leisurely crossed, and he appeared to be deeply engrossed in the middle of a book. Roger had a voracious appetite for reading. Despite his harmful and ofttimes belligerent behavior, he was an intelligent man. To the man's right, a meticulously made bed without a single wrinkle along the blanket's top surface. To his left was a closed door that opened into a small bathroom. As far as rooms went, it was more spacious than some of the cheaper motels in the area.

"You don't have to go in there, Miss Z," Tremont stated. "Ain't nothing you can say to that man that will change him from being who he is."

"And who is that, exactly, Tremont?" Sylvie questioned.

"A bad man."

"That may be," Sylvie remarked, "but inside every bad person, there's some good. Just as inside every good person, there's some bad. Not everything in this world is black and white. There's a lot of gray."

"You'll have to excuse me for disagreeing with you, Miss Z. I've watched over this man for a lot of years. There's no white or gray in him; his soul is black."

"And isn't your soul just a little darker now for feeling that way?"

The attendant gave her a solemn glance, then bowed his chin to his chest.

"I'm sorry, Tremont," Sylvie said, placing her hand on the man's shoulder. "I didn't mean it as it sounded."

He nodded.

"You'll still watch out for me, won't you?" she added, smiling and motioning toward the doorknob.

"Of course I will, Miss Z," the attendant replied, opening the door for her.

"Wish me luck," were her final words before she stepped through the door, distracting Roger from his reading. Before the door closed behind her, Tremont shot Roger a nasty glare to let him know Sylvie was under his protection. Roger took note of it. Tremont was an ox of a man; a warning from him wasn't something you took lightly. Roger returned an acknowledging smirk as the door swung shut.

"Hello, Roger," Sylvie began.

"Doctor," Roger returned, nodding as he swiveled in his chair to face her. "I was wondering when you'd be along."

"You believed I'd meet with you after what you did?"

He smiled, "I counted on it."

Sylvie felt her skin crawl – less at his comment than at the devious smile he flashed, though she wasn't about to let him know that.

"Well, I'm here," she said, twisting her head to glance around the room for a second chair.

"You won't find one," Roger stated, standing from his chair. "Please, take this one." He slid it to her, then backed away to sit on the edge of his bed.

Sylvie pulled the chair several feet away from the patient to keep her distance. As much as she felt she needed to meet with him, she wasn't foolish enough to think it unnecessary to take precautions. She kept her eyes focused on the man as she sat down, her shoulders tense with apprehension. The room remained silent for several seconds, the air between them thick. Then, to dispel the awkwardness, Roger spoke up.

"You want to ask me why I did it, but you're uncomfortable being in here with me. Well, Doctor, I can tell you it was for this reason or another, but it won't make a difference. You see me as you wish to see me, and nothing I say will make you believe otherwise."

"Then help me to understand, Roger. Tell me what that episode out there was all about. I'm listening."

"I wasn't going to hurt the old hag if that's what you were worried about. I was only using her. She was merely a means to an end."

"And what end was that?" Sylvie asked. "To get yourself exiled to your room, isolated from everyone else? You're fortunate Dr. Prichard didn't recommend mechanical or chemical restraint."

"Believe me, Doctor," he replied, "there are worse punishments." He leaned forward, resting his arms on his thighs as he clasped his hands together. "What I did out there," he said in a hushed tone, nodding his head toward the door, "that was to wake you up."

"To wake me up?" she questioned.

"A warning, if you will."

"You're warning me now? Was that a threat? Should I be concerned?"

"From me? No. Well, I can't be certain. After all, you saw what happened to poor Greta out there."

"I saw you trying to harm her, yes."

Roger smiled.

"What's so funny, Roger?" Sylvie asked.

"That you still think it was me holding that weapon to Greta's neck."

"I hate to break the news to you, Roger, but it *was* you."

He stared intently at her. "Was it? Hmm, I suppose it was."

She tilted her head slightly and smirked. "I think we can dispense with the games, Roger. I understand that you and Greta got into an altercation some time ago. Could that have been the reason you targeted her today?"

"You think I targeted Greta?"

"Didn't you?"

"It's true, we've had our disagreements in the past, but no," he said, shaking his head. "She wasn't the one I was . . . 'targeting.'"

"Is that so? Then tell me what it was about."

"I needed to bring awareness; I needed a witness."

"Awareness? You wanted people to witness what you did?"

"Not people. Just . . , someone."

"So there was someone specific meant to witness that terrifying display?"

"Tell me, Doctor, were *you* terrified?"

The room became silent as Sylvie stared into her patient's eyes while she thought carefully about her answer.

"I was . . . fearful for Greta's safety," she replied.

"But not for your own?" he questioned.

"I had nothing to be afraid of."

"You have no idea," Roger whispered.

"What was that?" Sylvie inquired.

"You need to get away from this place before it's too late."

"Too late for what?"

"Before something bad happens to you."

Sylvie shook her head. "If you're trying to scare me, Roger, it won't work. Everyone here at Somerset needs help. I'm here to do what I can, but your recent behavior concerns me. Let's forget about me for a moment and focus on you. What is it that *you're* so worried about?"

"Oh, I'm not worried, Doctor. There's a worse fate in store for me. I've seen how this all plays out. You can't stop what's coming."

Sylvie glanced at her patient confusedly.

"Really, Roger? Do you insist on continuing this exchange? Okay then, if it will help, why don't you tell me what's coming?"

"That would be too easy, wouldn't it?" he replied ominously. "Let's just say that not everything

– or every*one* – is as they seem. Did you do your homework before coming to this fine establishment? How much do you know about your patients? What about your . . . coworkers? How well do you know them? Do you know about all the dirty little secrets they hide from you? More importantly, do they know of the secret you hide from *them*?"

Sylvie felt a chill run down her spine.

"That's twice now you've alluded that I'm holding onto a secret. Would you care to explain what you think this so-called 'secret' is?"

"Come now, Doctor. There's a reason you're here, isn't there? If you're unwilling to share, how can you expect me to come clean about what I know?"

"That's just it, Roger," she commented, her voice sounding agitated, "and you'll have to pardon my language, but you don't know shit. You're just trying to get under my skin. Well, I'm telling you now, I'm done. I'm done listening to your rants. If you don't want my help, there's nothing I can do. I won't waste my time when others are more willing to accept it."

She stood from her chair and took a few steps toward the door before stopping and turning to face Roger one last time, her head and eyes shifting from one wall to the next before landing on her patient.

"Enjoy your stay in this little hole of yours, Mr. Loomis," she spoke harshly. "You can stay here forever if that's your choice."

With those final words, Sylvie turned and exited the room. Standing watch outside the door, the large attendant displayed a shocked glance in her direction.

"Everything all right, Miss Z?" the big man asked. "I've never heard you upset before."

"I'm sorry you had to hear that, Tremont," she responded. "I guess I'm still a little on edge from earlier. There's only so much a person can take, you know? Perhaps I should have waited before I went in."

"I told you his soul was black," he replied.

She looked down, nodding, perhaps not wanting Tremont to notice the guilt in her eyes.

"Yeah," she said, continuing to nod in agreement. "Listen, I'd better go. I feel a headache coming on, and in my current frame of mind, I'm not sure I can be here anymore. I'll try to catch up with you tomorrow, okay?" She gave a slight wave of her hand as she slowly shuffled away.

"Sure thing, Miss Z."

As she distanced herself from Roger's room, Sylvie couldn't help but think how harsh she had been. She let the man get to her, something she swore would never happen. And whatever she hoped to accomplish, meeting with him in his room as she had, her outburst certainly didn't help her cause. It was all the talk of secrets that rattled her. She knew she had to stay positive.

He doesn't know anything about my life, she thought. *He can't.*

Her thoughts continued to wander as she turned the corner, almost colliding with Dr. Prichard, who was himself rounding the corner.

"Oh, Dr. Prichard," she gasped. "I was just coming to see you."

"Is it something urgent, Dr. Zcieveteveicz?" he snapped. "I have an appointment."

"No, it's, um . . . I was just going to let you know that I'm leaving early. Roger's nonsense has given me a headache."

"Oh, you just came from Mr. Loomis' room?" Dr. Prichard inquired. "Did you learn anything from him? About the incident from earlier today?"

"Nothing useful," she replied. "He just kept speaking gibberish."

"I see," Dr. Prichard stated, his eyes narrowing as he stared at her. "Well, don't let me keep you," he added. "Go home and get some rest. We wouldn't want anything to happen to you, would we? Good doctors are hard to find."

He gave her a half-hearted smile, then continued around the corner. She watched as he strode away, wondering about his odd reaction. What struck her the most was his comment about good doctors being hard to find.

Since when did he consider me a good doctor, she thought. *It must be the personal stuff he's going through. That must be it. Sure. Whatever. I've got my own stuff to worry about. I can't get sidetracked by his behavior.*

She shook her head to wipe the negative thoughts from her mind as she slowly strolled back toward the main entrance.

Tomorrow's another day, she thought. *I just need some rest to clear my head. Many of the patients here are delusional about one thing or another. Roger's no different. I won't let him rattle me. Everything's going to be fine. I can still make this work.*

Chapter 10

Comfort Zone

With her legs curled up in her favorite chair while sipping her tea, Sylvie stared at the moving images on the television screen. If someone were to ask what she was watching, she wouldn't be able to tell them - the local news perhaps, as she recalled hearing something about electrical storms approaching from the west. Though her body was seated comfortably at home, her thoughts had never left the confines of the hospital's cold walls.

The early departure had done some good, relieving her impending headache, but she couldn't help but reflect upon the day she'd had. Roger's disconcerting words weighed heavily on her mind. He was spouting things that didn't make sense but still had her questioning his motives. If she were to believe the man, the entire threat was a charade to

88

gain her attention, though it would seem Greta was not in on the farce.

But why would he do such a thing? she thought. *What did he have to gain? And why am I still dwelling on the rantings of a madman?"*

Sylvie rolled her eyes and took another sip of her tea, pondering the warning she had been given. Roger told her she needed to get out of there before it was too late but wouldn't provide any details other than to say something was coming. Was that supposed to scare her, or was it his roundabout way of saying he didn't like her and wanted her gone from the hospital? She realized there were too many questions left unanswered. And even far more were left unasked. She couldn't help that; Roger had found a way under her skin, and she felt she had no choice but to leave his room before one of them did something they would have regretted. But now, because of it, she was left in a daze.

She hadn't been home for more than two hours and could already tell it was going to be a rough night, the man's foreboding words lingering with her longer than she should have allowed. The questions she hadn't asked were suddenly coming to her in droves. Did she even want to learn the answers? If Roger told her, would she even believe him? Probably not. Still, it was odd that he'd asked her if she did her "homework" before going to Somerset. She did, of course, but only as much as she needed to. Once she'd learned the truth - that what she was after was within those walls - there was no need to dig further. She was where she needed to be. Was there more for her to find? Perhaps, but she never intended to be there as long as she had. Her plan, however, had proven to be more difficult than anticipated. Clearly, she hadn't thought it all out before joining the Somerset staff.

Sylvie shook her head as if trying to shake away the thoughts like images on an Etch A Sketch. If only it were that simple. If only she could wash away everything from her past. Well, maybe not everything. It was her complicated past, after all, that made her the determined woman she currently was. But she couldn't help wondering how different things could have been. Would her parents still be around if not for what had happened? It wasn't worth dwelling upon. She'd already done that for too many years. It was time to put all of that behind her and move forward. If she could only get her plans at the hospital back on track, she could finally do just that. But it wasn't only about her. She was there for the patients as much as herself. At least, that's what she continued to tell herself.

Enough of this, Sylvie thought, placing her tea on the side table. *I can't even keep my wandering thoughts from splintering in different directions.*

Slapping the cushioned armrests and determined to rein her thoughts back in, she unfolded her legs and pushed herself up from her chair to retrieve the notes she'd taken during her patient visits earlier in the day. She'd placed them on her bed, a routine she'd developed to ensure she had some "light" reading material at bedtime. It was more to distract her than anything else. If she didn't read them, she worried the nightmares would return. Studying the patients to learn their motivations was the only thing that helped. Why did they do what they did to get admitted to Somerset Psychiatric Institution? She didn't have all the answers and maybe never would, but just the same, it didn't quell her fascination.

Many of the patients under Sylvie's care suffered from severe psychological disorders. Some of those patients went undiagnosed for years until they were finally able to get the treatment they deserved. Others lived seemingly normal lives until something caused a sudden chemical change in their brains. It could have been a head injury, a traumatic event, a chemical imbalance, or even a bacterial infection left untreated for too long. She knew Roger's story and what he had endured as a child, but other patients weren't always as forthcoming. Greta and Mrs. Landry were two such patients.

She'd been trying to get both of them to open up about what they had done, but they continued to avoid the subject like the plague. Sylvie knew bits and pieces of their stories, having studied their case files during her first month of employment, but she believed having them convey the tragic events would go a long way toward their recovery.

At the very least, she felt it would help unburden them of the guilt they must have been holding onto. In the end, she could only do so much. The rest was up to her patients.

She scooped the notepad and patient folders from her bed, then trodded her way to the kitchen to grab a spoon from the dish strainer and the half-eaten pint of Haagen-Dazs from the freezer. She'd tucked it out of sight to discourage sudden urges every time she opened the door, but on this night, the delicious treat called to her, tired of its place behind the freezer-burned bag of store-brand frozen peas. If she was going to skip dinner in favor of studying her patients, it was the only way to go. Her hips wouldn't think so, but she was willing to take the risk.

She marched back to the living room and plopped herself back into the welcoming embrace of her chair (at least, while she could still fit). She rested the paperwork on her lap, a necessary delay while she popped the cover off the Cookies n' Cream and stabbed the spoon into the crystalline ice crusted along the top layer. She wasn't picky; it'd do. After shoveling a hefty mound into her eagerly awaiting maw, Sylvie placed the container on the side table and opened her pad, flipping the pages to her most recent notes. The first patient on her list for the evening was Mrs. Landry.

As she skimmed down the page, Sylvie's concentration wasn't on the words. The aftertaste of the ice cream may have had something to do with it, but it was more about her thoughts on what could have triggered such a sweet woman as Mrs. Landry to land her in the state's psychiatric hospital. It wasn't a pleasant story, at least not how it ended.

But what about how it began, Sylvie thought? *If I'm going to learn anything about the woman's current behavior, perhaps it's worth another look into her past.*

With that thought, she stared at the page and let her mind wander back to what she had previously learned through notes and conversation about the odd Mrs. Landry.

Chapter 11

Twisted Sister

"**C**ongratulations, Mrs. Landry," the nurse stated through an awkward smile while handing the new mother her twins.

"They're girls."

Gloria Landry gazed at her daughters, her shocked husband standing beside her hospital bed, staring in stunned silence. Then, she turned her confused look toward the nurse. "I... I don't understand."

That was how life began for unexpected twins Cassandra and Gertrude Landry. It was late August of 1951, and by early September of that same year, life hadn't gotten any easier for the sisters when they were abandoned on the doorstep of Our Lady of Faith Children's Orphanage. And so it would seem, even at an early age, for at least one of the Landry girls, being institutionalized was a pre-destined fate.

Living conditions at the orphanage weren't the best, but it wasn't the worst fate the girls could have endured. At least they were given a chance at life. By the time they were ten and passed over numerous times by would-be adopters, they'd been countlessly reminded how they could have ended up in a dumpster. It was mostly teasing by the other girls on their floor, but they knew the words were true. That didn't help to ease their pain. The twins were shuffled off to the St. Agnes Boarding School for "special" kids. That was a kind way of saying "unadoptable."

Treated like outsiders, even by those who shared the same unchosen fate, Cassandra and Gertrude mostly kept to themselves. The sisters were the best of friends and did everything together. Having little alternative, they played with the same toys, had tea with the same imaginary friends, and talked endlessly about their dreams. But being as inseparable as they were wasn't without its problems.

At thirteen, Gertrude had taken to writing letters to a pen pal she'd acquired through reading the letters pages of an Archie comic book. When she received replies, she'd often be secretive about them, keeping them from the curious eyes of her inquisitive sister. Cassandra knew of the letters, often catching Gertrude trying to keep them out of view while reading them.

"What are you reading, Trudy?" Cassandra would ask.

"Never you mind," was almost always Gertrude's reply, an expression used by Sister Catherine, one of the caretakers from the orphanage who often delivered the phrase when one of the young ladies would ask her a personal question.

"I know what it is. It's a letter from your boyfriend," Cassandra said teasingly.

"Shut up, Cassie!"

"Show it to me."

"No. I said never you mind."

"It's not fair," Cassandra complained. "You *have* to share."

"I *don't* have to share. It's none of your business."

"But I'm your sister; we've always shared everything."

"Well, we don't *have* to share everything. You can always write your own letter, you know. Gee whiz, Cassie. You have to start living your own life."

Gertrude realized how harsh the words were the moment they left her lips.

"Yeah, like *that's* going to happen."

Gertrude shot her sister a nasty glance.

As weeks and months followed, and Gertrude continued brushing her sister's feelings aside, Cassandra spent many of those days pouting, even when Gertrude would offer apologetic conversation. Eventually, Cassandra would get over her sister's unwillingness to share, just as Gertrude would eventually get over her secretiveness.

As the years passed, the sisters watched many of the other girls leave to go to new homes while they remained behind, unchosen, unloved by any family. It only made their bond with each other that much stronger. They vowed to always be there for one another, to remain together, no matter what.

It was late in their seventeenth year, while at the boarding school – then renamed Saint Sophia's Boarding School for Girls - that the twins' conversations quickly matured past their teen years. They knew they were soon aging out of the system and would often have serious discussions about their plans after "captivity," as Cassandra would call it.

"Are you nervous?" Cassandra asked.

"Why would I be?"

"You know they don't keep us here after we turn eighteen."

"We still have a couple of months."

"But then what?"

"Well then . . . then we'll .. ,"

"Are you finally going to meet Thomas?" Cassie interrupted excitedly.

"No," replied Trudy.

"Why not?"

"You know why not."

"But you two have been writing to each other for so long."

"So."

"So, he's obviously interested in you."

"It's fine," Trudy stated, her somber expression taking control of her face. "We can continue to write."

"Do you think he's going to continue to wait forever?"

"If he doesn't, then he doesn't."

"How can you say that? After all the times you've told me how you can't wait to get married?"

"It wasn't real, Cassie," Trudy expressed. "It can't happen."

"What are you talking about? Of course, it can happen. Don't you think you deserve to be happy?"

"And what about you, Cassie?"

"What about me?"

"We've been together for so long. It's always been the two of us. Even if it were possible – even if Thomas wanted to get married after he met me – that wouldn't be fair to you. Besides, we made a promise to stay together."

"Listen, even if you were to get married, it's not like you're suddenly losing a sister. You're never getting rid of me. So, stop worrying about me. I have to 'start living my own life,' remember?"

Trudy dipped her chin to her chest, recalling the hurtful words of their past.

"I'm sorry about that, Cassie. I didn't mean to hurt you. But the answer is still no. Now that's the end of it."

"But . . ,"

"Never you mind!" Trudy exclaimed.

But that *wasn't* the end of it. The arguments continued for weeks, often escalating into heated fights. The young women had become so stubborn that neither was willing to listen to the other, even after their eighteenth birthday when they were put out on the street with only enough money to last a few weeks. It was too bad; maybe things could have been different. Maybe one of them could have been happy. Maybe even both. But that wasn't how the twins' story ended.

Seven days after they left the boarding school, Cassandra Landry was dead, covered in blood. The only other person present, holding a knife and also covered in blood, was her twin sister, Gertrude.

Indulging in another spoonful of ice cream, Sylvie shook her head, perplexed by the sisters' unique dynamic. The file didn't contain any more information than that - only a single line at the bottom of the last page stating the dead sister's autopsy records had been sealed to protect the living sister.

What did Cassandra do that set Gertrude off? What would have made Gertrude want to kill her sister? Sylvie knew there had to be something more, but files dating back to the 1960s had long since been lost or destroyed. She only had the stories of a confused woman to go by, and unfortunately, Mrs. Landry only shared what Sylvie already knew.

Sylvie closed the folder and shuffled it to the bottom of the pile. Next on top: Greta Lambeau.

Now, she's an interesting one, Sylvie thought. *I hope I have enough ice cream.*

And with that delectable thought, she plunged the spoon back into the cardboard container and opened the folder.

Chapter 12

In All Her Glory

It had been almost a year since Sylvie watched one of Greta's on-screen performances. She had never heard of the actress before joining the staff at Somerset, but after learning of the woman's history, she couldn't help but search out the titles, only to be amazed at how many of the actress's movies were available. She recalled the first one she'd purchased on her streaming service, thinking how silly it would probably be but entertaining nonetheless. She remembered being pleasantly surprised at the woman's captivating performance. She had such charisma, such camera presence.

For a twenty-six-year-old actress in 1979, playing the lead role in a feature film must have been a dream come true. "Cast Aside" was Greta's third movie, and the one that was to catapult her into the Hollywood spotlight. Her agent, however, had other plans.

Henry Gaston was a struggling talent agent in New York City looking to make a quick name for himself but had been facing financial difficulties. There was very little in the way of talent walking through his door, and those who did were often expecting too much for what little talent they had. At the time, he had only three actors under contract, one of whom was a child star only interested in doing commercials. The other two, both adult males, were talented enough actors to get gigs in supporting roles, but nothing so grand that would make Henry a sought-after agent or any real cash. But that all changed the day Greta Lambeau walked through the front door of his small talent agency.

It was 1977, and Greta had, only three days earlier, stepped off the bus into the heart of the Big Apple, delivered there from her hometown of Mansfield, Ohio. She was twenty-four, a dark-haired, fresh-faced beauty, and highly naïve. She was a struggling stage actress, looking for work and hoping to make it big on Broadway. But for Greta, stage life was only a stepping stone. Her true dream was to act in movies. She'd always wanted to be on the big screen, to be an actress in Hollywood like the women she adored: Marilyn Monroe, Audrey Hepburn, and her favorite,

Greta Garbo (mainly because they shared the same name). And she was more than ready to begin her new life.

She responded to an ad in the paper placed by the Bright Horizon Talent Agency, which had been looking for "gifted young actors ready to fulfill their dreams." It only took Greta one audition for Henry to realize he had a star on his hands.

Henry immediately took an interest in Greta and showed his willingness to further her career, which was not necessarily for *her* benefit but for his own. Naïve to a fault and having no prior experience with an agent, Greta jumped at the opportunity to sign with Henry's Agency.

Henry Gaston was a decent enough agent, at least to those he felt could make him some money, and he worked tirelessly to promote his latest acquisition. He had a few connections with some small television studio producers and eventually convinced one of them to give his newest actress a try in a small television spot.

Greta's first acting job in the new city she now called home was a commercial for Dowery Cooking Spray. Though it didn't demonstrate her true talent, it was enough of a spotlight to get her a second job: a recurring stint as a waitress in a short-lived television show. It was a minor role, and the program, which failed to live up to viewer's expectations, was canceled after only five episodes, but the buzz around the local studio was all about how an unknown actress from Ohio outperformed the other, more experienced cast members. Henry was only seeing dollar signs whenever he looked at his newest acquirement.

By the end of 1977, after several small roles in mildly successful daytime dramas, Greta was cast in her first major motion picture. It was a small role as a supporting actress behind the lead, but it was her first "big" break. It was during that shoot of "Streets of Despair" that Greta and Henry began a romantic, perhaps even questionable relationship, and it was during the beginning stages of that relationship when Henry would get his first hint of the dark secret Greta had been holding onto.

He noticed the scars on her abdomen and upper thighs during their second sexual encounter (Greta insisted on leaving the lights off during their first). When questioned about them, Greta brushed them aside as having had an accident that left her slightly scraped up, and she quickly changed the subject. Having no reason to doubt her word, Henry disregarded his initial concerns about them.

By June of 1978, Henry managed to book Greta a more prominent movie role where she would play alongside Burt Reynolds as his character's love interest. A few months before the start of production was to begin, however, Burt Reynolds was forced to back out of the role due to scheduling conflicts. A lesser-known actor was cast in his place, and the movie, "Winner Takes It All," failed to capture audiences. The one uplifting note for Henry was that critics praised Greta's performance, noting that the actress was the one bright spot in an otherwise dull film. The praises, however, did nothing to build Greta's self-esteem.

Failing to make an impact, even with the support of her agent and boyfriend, Greta began doubting her acting abilities, turning to alcohol and other external means to help alleviate her growing depression. She had frequent outbursts and often displayed sudden and extreme mood swings. Almost immediately, Henry noticed the newer scars appearing on Greta's personage, interspersed among the scars and scabs of the old. It was then that he understood.

Though it would come out much later during her trial that Greta had been previously diagnosed with Borderline Personality Disorder and that the harm she inflicted upon herself was one way she coped with the negative reviews and lackluster ticket sales of her movies, at the time, Henry had no idea the severity of Greta's mental health disorder.

Not wanting any harm to befall his budding star, which, in turn, could negatively impact his financial gain, Henry insisted Greta seek professional help for her self-harming ways. Though a nasty argument ensued, she ultimately agreed, realizing her compliance would continue to gain her more roles and further her career.

It would be the later testimony of noted psychiatrist Dr. Conroy Tipton that chiefly played a role in the judge's decision to have Greta committed to a psychiatric institution for further evaluation – and later still, her long stay at Somerset. But in late 1978, it was business as usual, and Henry scored Greta her first leading role in an upcoming feature film.

The low-budget movie "Cast Aside," Greta's third feature film, was released in September of 1979 to critical acclaim due to Greta's unparalleled performance as Maggie Deetweiler, a strong-willed prostitute who later abandoned the sex industry to found an organization dedicated to finding homes for wayward children. Poignant and heartfelt, the movie had an impact on all those who watched Greta breathe life into the unforgettable character. And Hollywood, too, took notice.

Seemingly overnight, the offers suddenly began pouring in from larger studios, wanting to cast Greta in their latest blockbusters, but Henry feared what his client's instant fame could mean. By that time, the couple's personal relationship had already become tumultuous, at best, and as much as he wished Greta great success, which continued to bolster his bank account, he realized a move to Hollywood could put a strain on their *professional* relationship as well.

Henry was a one-man show and under no pretense. He knew that the shiny allure of Tinseltown could easily sway his star client into signing a multi-deal contract with a larger agency. They had more connections, more clout, and a handful of law firms on retention that would find loopholes in his contract, enabling them to cut him out of the picture entirely. They could bury him in legal fees before a fight even began. He wasn't about to let that happen. He turned away offer after offer, explaining to Greta that the roles being promised her weren't good enough to showcase her extraordinary talent.

To keep her distracted, Henry continued to book Greta movie deals with smaller, independent studios. But with each new role, the offers from the bigger Hollywood studios became less and less, until eventually, they ceased altogether.

Though the movies she was making were all quite good, without the financial backing of the major studios, they failed to make their way into larger theaters, limiting her exposure to audiences. Greta sank further into depression, and her extreme mood swings returned - with them, her urge to cut herself.

By 1985, with Hollywood offers having dried up, Greta felt she had no alternative but to remain with Henry and his little agency. She had starred in a string of grade-B movies that hadn't amounted to much except to increase the bitterness she felt for her agent and manager. Her alcohol and drug abuse had spun out of control, and her self-harm tendencies had consumed her. She was an empty shell of the actress she once was, spiraling deeper into despair.

In February of 1986, during the filming of "Tainted Heart," what would become Greta's final movie, Henry walked into the actress's RV to find she was cutting herself with a razor blade - the first time he'd ever witnessed the act.

According to Greta's later testimony, her manager became enraged and began screaming at her, threatening to throw her back on the street where he'd found her "no-talent ass." Things became a bit confusing in the transcript later released by the courts. Greta had stated Henry struck her several times while in her trailer, yet there was no physical evidence to support such a claim.

According to her testimony, when she held out the razor defensively to stop his attacks, he angrily lunged at her. She remembered closing her eyes, waiting for an assault that, surprisingly, never came. When she opened her eyes, Henry was on his knees, gurgling and grasping his neck while blood streamed down his fingers. His neck had been sliced.

Greta testified that she cried out for help several times, but nobody on set recalled hearing any screaming. She didn't attempt to call 911 for emergency medical help, and when somebody eventually checked on her, the only signs of physical abuse were the self-inflicted cuts along her side. Though some things about the incident could have been easily argued, two things that could not were that Henry died of his wounds in Greta's trailer and that she was the one who held the bloody blade.

It was a speedy trial, and although Greta's attorney argued that his client acted purely in self-defense and that Mr. Gaston's death, although tragic, was an unfortunate accident, Greta's past sessions with Dr. Tipton presented her in a different light. Her Borderline Personality Disorder often caused Greta to become unstable. Most of the time, her aggression was directed inward at herself, displayed in the many scars engraved in her flesh. The doctor argued that, in his professional opinion, Greta was also a manic depressive, and those same self-aggressive behaviors could cause her to lash out violently toward others. In the case of Henry Gaston, Greta felt threatened and lashed out at the person she believed had gotten in the way of her success. The incident might never have happened had Henry not walked in on her during one of her depressive episodes. He was simply in the wrong place at the wrong time.

Sylvie shook her head and closed the manila folder on her lap. There wasn't anything more in those papers that would gain her further insight into Greta Lambeau. Anything new would have to come from the failed actress herself, and like Mrs. Landry, she wasn't talking.

Sylvie glanced over at the container of half-melted ice cream and quietly groaned. She had gotten too caught up in Greta's file to notice its worsening condition. It was just as well; she didn't need the extra calories. Not to mention, her eyes were becoming heavy, and eating more of the sugary treat would only succeed in waking her in the middle of the night. She'd rather leave that distinction to her troubled thoughts, of which she had many. For now, she'd save her hips and put away the unforgiving dessert that was currently more milkshake than ice cream. She was ready to turn in for the night and hope for the best. Or, at least, hope *not* for the worst.

Chapter 13

The Bad Man

She could have used a few more hours of sleep. That was a luxury long gone since her late teens. She'd given up on sleeping pills. They induced the nightmares - the nightmares of *him*. The bad man. She hoped that would change after she accomplished her goal, though she had no idea how long that would be or if it was even possible. But that's why she was at Somerset - to find a way to make them stop.

The drive to work was bleak during the early morning hours, the clouds stampeding in like thunderous horses, threatening rain. The morning radio personality confirmed the incoming storm during the hourly weather update. Some areas along the outskirts of the city were already experiencing power outages. She had a feeling it was going to be a fierce one.

It wasn't often Sylvie found herself going to work early, but with her mind still racing from the previous day's events, she welcomed the distraction it would bring. She also hoped for an opportunity to meet with Roger again. She didn't like the way they had left things. She wouldn't apologize for her unprofessionalism - lord knew the man didn't deserve that - but perhaps she could tolerate his behavior long enough to get some answers.

She pulled into the entrance between the two six-foot decorative brick towers by the roadside, reading the tarnished silver placards on each as she always did while driving through. The left tower's placard displayed the numbered address, 1670. The right displayed the facility's name, the word "SOMERSET" in large letters on the top line, distracting a reader from noticing the words "Psychiatric Institution" in much smaller letters underneath. It was as if the very thought of a psych ward was a blight on the community.

After the lonely trip along the property's lengthy private drive, Sylvie pulled into the scarcely populated parking lot along the east wing. Her attention became immediately drawn to a particular vehicle. The black and silver Porsche 911, Dr. Prichard's pride and joy, was impossible to miss. He kept his shiny toy in pristine condition, and though the lot was mostly empty, he parked far away from the other vehicles to avoid possible dents or scratches. She thought about parking her old, barely driveable Hyundai Tucson next to it as a joke, but the passive statement would most likely go unnoticed by the egotistical doctor. Not to mention, it would only succeed in making Sylvie feel depressed about where her life was in comparison. She decided to park several rows away from the overly-priced status symbol. At the very least, it was healthier for her frame of mind.

That aside, she wondered why the doctor was there on a Friday. It wasn't like him to grace the hospital with his presence more than once a week unless there was a special board meeting, and even that would take place at a later hour than five-thirty in the morning. As she strolled along the walkway to the front entrance, she tried counting the number of times she'd seen him at the hospital on a day other than Thursday but struggled to make it past the first four digits on her left hand.

Whatever it was, she thought, *there must be a good reason.*

Sylvie abruptly stopped at the large sliding doors, expecting them to open as always. It was way too early in the morning for her to have to think, and she'd forgotten the entrance remained locked until Glen or Jules arrived at 6:30 to start their morning shift. Sighing heavily in frustration, she rummaged through her jacket pocket to retrieve her badge. She could have knocked on the glass until security was alerted to her presence and buzzed her in, but they frowned upon that practice since the scanners were in place to log each staff member's entrance.

Pulling the badge from her pocket, Sylvie swiped it in front of the scanner to open the large vestibule doors into the empty waiting area, catching the attention of Venessa, the on-duty security guard, who looked up from reading her book.

"Do my eyes deceive me?" Venessa acknowledged. "Well, hello there, stranger. I haven't seen you in weeks, Sylvie. What brings you here at such an ungodly hour?"

"I'm asking myself that same question," Sylvie replied. "I couldn't stop thinking about yesterday. Did you hear what happened?"

"You mean Roger?"

"The one and only."

"Everyone was talking about it," Venessa said, flipping her book upside down to preserve her page. "It's not like it's the first time he's acted up. Although it has been a while since his last episode."

"Since before I started working here," Sylvie responded. "I'm actually surprised I hadn't seen that behavior before yesterday."

"Why is that?"

"You know, because of his past. I guess I expected his violent tendencies to surface sooner."

"Consider yourself lucky, honey. You haven't had to deal with the worst of Roger Loomis. Medications are glorious – until they stop working."

Sylvie hesitated before nodding. "Yeah, lucky," she said before glancing around her. "So, why are you here and not Ricardo? Did you two switch shifts?"

"We've been without Ricardo for a few weeks now," Venessa replied. "I've been pulling double shifts since."

"Did they fire another one? I feel like I'm so out of the loop."

"Oh, you didn't hear? He fell off his roof and broke both his legs."

"Oh no. How awful."

"Yeah, but I'm not complaining; it's been nice here without him. And the extra money has been helping out a lot. I feel bad for you first-shifters, though; you've still got to deal with 'Guard Dog.'"

"He's not that bad."

"You only say that because you don't have to deal with his ragged ass when he first gets in," Venessa responded.

"That's true. Speaking of getting in . . , I noticed Dr. Prichard's car in the lot. When did he get here?"

"He got here a little over an hour ago. Third day in a row."

"*Third* day?" Sylvie inquired. "You mean he was here on Wednesday, too?"

"Sure was - about the same time as this morning."

"That's strange."

Venessa placed her elbow on the window's shelf, her arm vertical, and propped her chin into her open palm. "Sylvie, I don't know if you're aware of this, but you work in a psych hospital; there's nothing *but* strange around here."

Sylvie rolled her eyes. "Haha. Funny," she said sarcastically. "Listen, it's been good talking with you, Venessa, but I'd better get inside before that ragged guard dog you spoke about gets here."

"Good thinking."

Sylvie flashed her badge in front of the scanner at the interior door, but the door didn't open. Without thinking anything of it, she tried a second time. The door remained closed, adding to her continued frustration. After an unsuccessful third attempt, she turned to alert Venessa of her troubles.

"I think there's something wrong with my badge, Venessa. It doesn't seem to be working."

"Oh, it's not you," Venessa responded. "We've been having trouble with that damn thing for a while. Jules tells me it works fine during the day. That may be true, but it's shit at night. I don't get it."

"Electrical?"

"The hell if I know. The only electricity I know about is the kind I make when I get home and crawl into bed with my wife - if you know what I mean." Venessa smirked while rapidly raising and lowering her eyebrows.

Sylvie smiled uncomfortably. "Yeah, I got it. No details are necessary. Would you mind buzzing me in?"

"Sure thing."

Venessa's hand slipped under the shelf, a faint buzz sounded, and the interior doors slid open.

"Thanks, Venessa," Sylvie said, putting her hand up in a subtle wave as she walked through the door. "Good seeing you."

The door slid closed behind her as she walked left toward the staircase leading to the lower floor. She wanted to drop her things in her office and check any messages she might have had before visiting with Roger. She knew he'd be awake. The man boasted of waking at four each morning so he could get some quiet reading time in before having to "deal with all the noise," as he'd stated many times, though with him being confined to his room and having nothing *but* quiet time to fill his day, perhaps he decided to sleep later. She was willing to take her chances. He was a creature of habit and probably more awake at that hour than she was.

She descended the stairs into the darkened corridor, the annoying fluorescent light flickering on and off, still clinging to the last of its life. She had asked to have it replaced, along with a second one farther down the hall that had burned out long before, but with the maintenance crew overhauling the "new" kitchen facilities on the first floor (the hospital was too cheap to hire outside contractors), it was understandable how the lights in the basement could easily fall off their already-overworked radar. She would have done it herself weeks earlier if there was a step ladder handy. Until such time, however, she was forced to suffer with the blinking annoyance. She was thankful she didn't have to spend much time in her personal dungeon.

The "lower floor," as the rest of the staff insisted on calling it (Sylvie wasn't so naïve; she knew it was the hospital's basement), was quiet, consisting of only two offices, an old file room, a single-stall bathroom, and a small janitorial closet. Sylvie's office had previously been located at the end of the hall just left of the staircase until the former staff psychologist quit, allowing Sylvie to relocate to the newly emptied office closer to the stairwell. They hadn't backfilled the position since, making Sylvie the lone resident on the deserted floor. But as she inserted her key into her door's lock, she heard a loud scraping sound coming from the far end of the corridor, making her believe she *wasn't* alone. She glanced toward the vacant office but found herself only staring into darkness.

"Hello?" she called out, letting the keys dangle from the knob.

She listened for a moment, hearing only her breath becoming shallower.

"Is someone down there?" she questioned, straining her eyes to see the farther office door.

Though the lower floor was openly accessible to the hospital's staff, others would rarely descend into the bowels of the facility. There was no reason to; everything they needed was on the main floor. Still, something down the hall made a noise. She didn't imagine it. Or did she? It was still early, and she *was* tired. Her mind could've been playing tricks on her like it used to years before when she'd stare into the shadows, waiting for the "bad man" to come and take her. He never did, and she thought she'd finally gotten over that irrational fear. Yet, there she stood, looking for something that wasn't there and only imagining the worst.

This is ridiculous, she thought, the hair on her arms still pulling at her skin. *Of course, it was nothing. I'm just on edge.* And as she continued to stare in the direction she'd heard the scraping, her thoughts reflected on young Kevin's words.

You're the only person I know who doesn't have a cell phone.

She could have used one at the moment. She wasn't interested in calling anyone, but the convenience of a light would have been handy.

She called out again, perhaps expecting different results.

"Is anyone there?"

Isn't that the definition of insanity? She thought. *Well, at least I'm in a psych hospital.* The thought of comic relief did nothing to ease her mind. She knew her fear would prevent her from stepping into her office, where she'd be trapped inside with no means to escape should someone bust in and block her exit. Would she be able to dial for help fast enough? Would anyone even hear her muffled screams? No, she knew she'd need to satisfy her curiosity. She also knew it was why most people died in horror movies, foolishly investigating strange noises when they should've been running away instead.

This isn't a movie, she thought. *Just get on with it.* And with that unenthusiastic thought motivating her, she apprehensively stepped toward the vacant office. Her eyes slowly adjusted to the darkness, at least as much as they could, so she knew there was nobody between her and the door. The noise she heard could have been coming from inside. With her mind racing and heart pounding, she reached for the knob, but before she could grab onto it, something from behind her grabbed her shoulder instead.

Letting out a sharp scream as she jumped and spun around, Sylvie's back slammed against the office door.

"Dr. Zcieveteveicz," a voice spoke out. "You're a bit jumpy this morning."

It was Dr. Prichard, smirking smugly, a few file folders tucked under his arm.

"Shit!" Sylvie exclaimed, placing her hand on her chest. "I guess I am."

"I can see why," the psychiatrist stated, pointing to the overhead light fixtures. "We should get someone down here to replace these lights."

"Maybe you'll have better luck with that than I've had," she replied. She glanced at the folders tucked into the doctor's armpit. "What brings you down here, doctor?"

"Oh, nothing so exciting, I'm afraid. I was in the old file room, reviewing a few older cases I'd had. I thought there might be something useful for some of my current patients. That's when I heard you call out. I was surprised to see you by your old office. It's been empty since Evelyn left; did you forget something?"

"No, I thought I heard something. It's silly, I know, but I was checking it out."

"I'm not surprised," Dr. Prichard responded. "Old buildings like this are always creaking and popping. We should look into having maintenance build you a space upstairs. Maybe a small area of the old kitchen can be portioned off and turned into a new office space."

Sylvie's eyes lit up. "That . . . that would be great."

"After the new kitchen is complete and fully operational, of course," he added.

Sylvie's shoulders dropped with disappointment. "Right."

The old kitchen was in shambles, with plastic sheeting draped from the ceiling at the entryway to act as a barrier, and had remained untouched for months while maintenance poured what little resources they had into the new kitchen. With maintenance having to work around the kitchen staff's schedule, who were themselves burdened with having to work in a half-renovated kitchen, it was a slow process. Not to mention, with everything else in the facility that needed attention, it would still be weeks before the new kitchen was ready, and then, it would be even more weeks before they got around to clearing out the *old* kitchen. After that, how long would it take to build a new office? It wasn't a promising thought.

"Until then, I'm afraid," the doctor continued, "you'll have to endure the strange noises. Don't let them get to you, Sylvie. There's nothing to be afraid of."

Dr. Prichard smirked, then turned and walked away. She watched as the white of his lab jacket brightened and dimmed with the flickering of the fluorescent light. She wondered if he'd meant for his last comment to be as sarcastic and condescending as it sounded. It wouldn't surprise her. The man was an arrogant ass who probably believed all women were scared and weak. The current circumstance aside, where she had let her thoughts get the best of her, she was neither scared nor weak. It was only a matter of time before the doctor realized that. Regardless, as Dr. Prichard's form disappeared from the top of the stairwell, Sylvie turned back to the office door, determined to wash away any worry. This time, with her fear suppressed to the back of her mind, she grabbed the knob and quickly opened the door. Nothing immediately jumped at her as she flipped the light switch on. That was encouraging. The empty office was as one would expect. There was a cleared-off desk, with only a phone on it, in the center of the floor. The front of the desk was open enough in the middle to see nobody was hiding under it. Against the front wall stood an empty bookcase, while a row of three filing cabinets occupied the far wall behind the desk. As Dr. Prichard stated, there was nothing to be afraid of.

Sylvie let out a heavy sigh of relief and closed the door behind her. And as she quickly walked back to her office, a single thought entered her mind.

See, Sylvie? No bad man.

Chapter 14

Scribbles

Her day had only just begun, and it was already shaping up to be an unusual morning. Sylvie knew it would get worse before it got better. After all, she still had her interview with Roger to look forward to. For now, however, even though she disliked the lower floor, she'd take the alone time to gather herself before then. She'd gotten worked up over nothing, a feeling only exacerbated by Dr. Prichard sneaking up on her. The entire situation was peculiar.

Dr. Prichard mentioned he was in the old file room, looking through some older case files. She'd never taken the opportunity herself. She never felt the need. None of her former patients from her previous employ had ever stayed at Somerset. She hadn't planned on staying herself. So, to her, it was just another room in the basement that people had forgotten about.

Well, apparently not everyone, she thought. Still, Dr. Prichard's sudden interest in the files piqued her curiosity. *Was that why he'd been there so early the last three days?* she wondered. *What was he researching?*

Though she'd only been at Somerset a little over a year and a half, she had never seen anyone researching old patient files. She wasn't sure how they would be relevant. She did recall hearing a few stories from other staff members about some of the former patients, but they were from long ago, and she couldn't be sure how true they were. People often embellished the narrative for dramatic purposes. And, of course, she could have easily found out the truth by exploiting the use of the room, but she felt uncomfortable about it. But now that she'd personally witnessed a senior colleague make use of the files, perhaps she would reconsider her stance on the subject. Convincing herself that perusing the old files would aid in distracting her from her gnawing anxiety, she stood from her desk and exited into the strobing hallway.

The old file room was back toward the staircase, then down the corridor in front of it. She'd only ever gone down that hallway to use the bathroom, which was located directly across from the file room door. Just past the bathroom, on the right, there was a small janitor's closet that housed a nasty old mop and bucket that looked like it hadn't been used in a decade, a couple of empty cans of Comet cleaner, and a broom with its handle broken in half. The hallway itself extended farther but didn't lead anywhere except to a cinderblock wall. It was a strange layout. She'd been told by the former basement-dwelling resident that the entire floor had been much larger at one time. It'd been home to the old surgical room where they used to perform lobotomies before it was closed off a dozen or so years earlier when the hospital had added the new wing. Whatever the case, it was creepy as hell.

She stood at the door to the file room, staring at the electronic scanner while pulling her badge from her pocket, wondering if she even had access to the room. She swiped her badge across the face of it and watched the red light flicker off, then on again. She was initially disappointed by the result, questioning why she wouldn't have access. But, as she often did when unable to accept an unfavorable outcome, she swiped a second time and watched with satisfaction as the red light turned green.

Weirdly, like a child on Christmas morning, Sylvie felt a hint of excitement when she pulled the lever handle down and the door cracked open. It was like she was sneaking into a place she wasn't allowed.

Nervously, she opened the door a little wider, and the overhead light, which was motion-activated, briefly flickered on and off before fully illuminating the small room.

Why can't they install those in the hallway, she thought as she poked her head into the opening to peer around the door, curious about the room's layout.

It was smaller than she expected, smaller even than her office. There were eight standing, four-drawer filing cabinets along three walls. Two were against the wall directly behind the door, which prevented it from swinging open more than ninety degrees. Two other cabinets were centrally located along the adjacent wall on the left, allowing for only enough space for the cabinets against the first wall to open. Then, the remaining four cabinets resided against the wall opposite the door. The right wall was bare, which allowed entry into the room. Had Sylvie been claustrophobic, the quick peek inside would have ended her curiosity. She hadn't such a fear (hers was much darker), so she stepped inside and quickly closed the door as if concerned someone would notice her entering. It was a strange thought, considering her motives for wanting to work at Somerset in the first place. Nevertheless, she remained cautious.

Stepping in front of the first set of cabinets behind the door, she scanned the handwritten labels affixed to each drawer. From top to bottom, the drawers were labeled sequentially by date, starting with 1973. She skipped the first four cabinets, deeming any file older than she was unnecessary to peek at. She jumped right to 1989, curious about what the patients were like when she was only four years old.

Flipping through the folders, she landed on Paul Eckert, a disturbed young man who killed his parents, claiming they had become possessed by Satan. That folder quickly went back into its spot.

Sylvie jumped ahead to 1994, where the folder of Jessica Tartikauf grabbed her attention. The woman was a patient at Somerset for killing her three sons. She believed they had turned into werewolves and were threatening to eat her. Though there had indeed been a full moon the night of the incident, the judge rightfully dismissed the claims and, at the recommendation of the lawyers and medical professionals on the case, had Jessica committed for psychotic paranoid schizophrenia.

Digging deeper into the cabinets, Sylvie opened the drawer labeled 2002. She plucked a random folder with the name Stuart Clark listed on the top tab. Shuffling through the pages within, she learned Stuart had previously been in and out of the Teton Psych Hospital for mild delusional behavior. He believed he was the starting first baseman for the 1902 Boston Americans, a team that would later become the Boston Red Sox. According to the notes of Dr. Charles Spiney, Teton's resident psychiatrist at the time, Stuart's behavior, although delusional, was harmless and easily treatable with regularly scheduled therapy sessions. At Dr. Spiney's recommendation, Stuart was released from Teton on his own recognizance with explicit orders from the judge that he continue his therapy with the doctor at his private residence. The sessions took place as mandated, and on the morning of April 19th, 2002, Stuart arrived at the doctor's residence for what would be his final session. He carried with him a baseball bat, and when Dr. Spiney answered the door, Stuart struck him in the head, knocking him back from the entrance. Stuart then calmly entered the home and proceeded to beat both the doctor and his wife with the bat until their bodies lay a bloody mess on the floor. When taken into custody, Stuart was ranting about how his manager asked him to take batting practice before the game. After all, it was April 19th, the opening day for the 1902 Boston Americans. Stuart was sentenced to Somerset indefinitely but died two years later of an inoperable brain tumor, which may have been the cause of his delusions.

Sylvie shook her head at the minimal amount of files she'd sampled, wondering if they were all as bad. She didn't know if reading them was helping soothe her anxiety or contributing to it. She decided to abandon the idea of continuing and filed Stuart Clark away. As she went to close the drawer, however, her eyes spotted a folder labeled "Roger Loomis." Her initial thought was that it was either mislabeled or filed incorrectly since the files in the basement were of Somerset's *former* patients. Thinking to rectify the mistake, Sylvie pulled the folder from the drawer and opened it to determine which. It never occurred to her that there might be a third option.

The pages within were dated 1997 through 2003, the duration of Roger's stay at Teton Psychiatric Hospital.

What is this doing here, Sylvie thought as she flipped through the documents, noticing the unusual scribbled phrases such as "subject responding negatively to dosage," and "treatment resulting in unexpected behavior." Other words caught her eye, too, such as "Ditrolazipan Sulfate" and "experimental drug." Page after page, handwritten notes regarding "subject" and "trial" were prevalent. "Subject exhibiting violent tendencies." "Trial 17 inconclusive." "Subject ready for trial 21." Sylvie couldn't believe what she was reading. None of it made any sense. Why was the folder even there? It was a question she couldn't answer, but as she flipped to the last page, she suddenly realized who could.

The signature was unmistakable. Sylvie herself had once commented on the unique flair the person had when signing his name. Dr. Thadeus Prichard took great pride in his signature - more so than he did with the rest of his barely-legible scribbling.

But this is a file from Teton, Sylvie thought. *I didn't know Dr. Prichard worked there.*

Just then, the overhead light flashed and went out, and Sylvie froze for several seconds, holding onto the open cabinet drawer to keep her bearings.

She closed her eyes, squeezed them tightly shut, and took in a deep breath to keep herself calm and focused. When she reopened them seconds later, the light had returned. She let out a heavy breath in relief and quickly shut the drawer.

Stupid power outages, she thought as she reached for the door handle to make her way out. She didn't return the folder, choosing instead to keep it with her so she could question Dr. Prichard about its significance.

Maybe the negative thoughts swirling around in her head were all wrong. Maybe there wasn't anything unusual about what she'd read. Experimental drug trials were common practice, especially in years past. Pharmaceutical companies depended on them. Then again, what if her thoughts *weren't* wrong? What if Roger had been a lab rat, part of some twisted experimentation? Was he a willing participant? Did he know what they were doing to him? Either way, Roger was now a patient under her care, and she aimed to find out what everything in that folder meant.

Chapter 15

Who's to Blame

Gathering her wits about her, Sylvie marched up the stairway, Roger Loomis' file firmly gripped between her fingers. It was clear the file she held had some unusual information within. If her suspicions were correct, it was information others weren't knowledgeable about. Well, others except for one.

Dr. Prichard's signature was on the medical notes. He was the practicing Psychiatrist at Teton Psychiatric Hospital during Roger's stay, something Sylvie was unaware of until she happened upon the folder. The doctor had neglected to share that fact with her during her year-and-a-half employment. Not that it was necessary (perhaps a welcome courtesy, however). What was most disconcerting about the documents were the doctor's notes about the patient and the bizarre "treatment" being subjected to him. It read like some science experiment; she wasn't sure what to make of it. That was why she intended to confront Dr. Prichard with her findings. She wondered if the subject matter had anything to do with the circumstances behind Roger's transfer to Somerset. She only hoped he would share the information.

As Sylvie reached the top of the staircase and rounded the corner, she noticed the light penetrating through the front sliding doors, the sun's defiant rays having successfully battled the darkening clouds. Daylight had shown its face, and it brought with it a shift change.

The ever-perky Jules had now taken her place at the front desk, and Glen had relieved Venessa of her nightly watch. Sylvie walked by the large glass entryway, noticing the "Guard Dog" outside again, which seemed to be his favorite spot. She stopped at the receptionist's door just past the vestibule and peered into the small, square, reinforced glass window where she could see Jules writing notes in the hospital's logbook. She rapped two knuckles against the glass to gain Jules' attention. When the smiling attendant looked up, Sylvie gave her a quick head nod and waved. Jules returned an overly excited wave of her own, paired with an exaggerated smile from ear to ear. Sylvie wished she had as much enthusiasm for *her* job.

She continued forward, scanning her badge at the steel door that led into the doctors' offices. As Sylvie passed by Dr. Lee's open door on her way to see Dr. Prichard, she noticed him stand from his desk and point in her direction.

"Oh, Sylvie," he called out, causing her to pause just past his doorway. "Can I talk with you for a moment?"

"Can it wait?" she replied. "There's something I need to see Dr. Prichard about."

"Dr. Prichard's left already," he responded. "I saw him pulling out as I was pulling in."

"Oh. Shit."

Dr. Lee glanced down at the file Sylvie was holding, then back to her eyes.

"Something I can help you with?" he offered.

"Oh, ah, no," she stumbled, sliding the file slightly behind her leg, not because she shouldn't have had it, but because she didn't want to talk to Dr. Lee about it. At least, not until she'd spoken with Dr. Prichard first. "You said you wanted to speak with me?"

"Yes, I did. I thought you should know that whatever you spoke about in your sessions with Greta and Mrs. Landry yesterday seemed to spark some enthusiasm. After you left, both ladies had nothing but good things to say about their discussion with you."

"Really?" Sylvie replied, unconvinced.

"Yeah. They said they couldn't wait for their next meeting with you. They said it was sure to be one you'd appreciate."

"That's odd."

"Well, maybe. But whatever it is you're doing, it seems to be effective. Keep up the good work."

"Okay, thank you. I will."

Dr. Lee smiled as his eyes wandered back down to the file Sylvie was holding.

"Are you sure there's nothing I can help you with?" he asked again, pointing to the file.

She looked down at the manila folder and let her tense shoulders drop. It wasn't what she'd planned, but maybe talking with the doctor would help alleviate some concerns.

"Maybe you can," she began, opening the file and handing it to her colleague. "What do you make of this?"

Dr. Lee quickly skimmed the first page, then lifted it to scan the second.

"Where did you get this?" he asked, a confused look on his face.

"It was in the old file room downstairs."

"The old file room? Do people still go in there?"

"Apparently, Dr. Prichard does," Sylvie answered. "He pulled some files from there just this morning. It made me curious, so I checked it out for the first time. That's when I found this file on Roger."

"Okay," Dr. Lee shrugged, confused. "Besides it being weird that anyone would check out those old files, what am I supposed to be looking at here?"

"These are notes from Roger's time at Teton," she expressed.

"Well, it's not unusual to have patient files transferred to us, Sylvie. You know that."

"No, I get that," Sylvie replied. "Just take a look at some of the medical notes." She tapped her index finger on the text in the middle of the page on sheet two.

Dr. Lee read to the bottom of the page, his expression showing mild puzzlement.

"I do admit some of the notes seem a bit unusual," he remarked. "But Roger was at Teton a long time ago. That was before my time here. And who knows what any of this means?"

"I can tell you who knows," Sylvie jumped in, pulling the pages up to show Dr. Lee what she'd found. "Right there," she said, pointing to the bottom of the last page.

Dr. Lee looked more confused, then looked back to Sylvie.

"That's Dr. Prichard's signature," he said. "I didn't know he worked at Teton."

"That's not all," Sylvie responded. "His notes indicate that Roger was given some sort of experimental drug – Ditrolazipan Sulfate – on the morning of August 6th, 2003. Have you ever heard of that? It states it was 'trial 26.'"

"No, I haven't," Dr. Lee replied. "But what's so significant about the date?"

"That was the same day Roger attacked that young intern. It's what got him transferred out of Teton."

"Wow, you certainly know more about Roger than I do."

"I . . . make a habit of learning about all my patients," she replied. "But don't you find that to be odd? The notes state Roger was exhibiting violent behavior because of the treatments, and then he attacked that young woman on the very day he'd been administered 'trial 26.'"

"Coincidental, maybe," Dr. Lee answered, "but odd..? I mean, we don't know what that drug was. For all we know, it was a placebo. I'm sure Dr. Prichard knew what he was doing. Besides, there's nothing in here that indicates Roger's violent behavior was directly caused by the drug, just that he was exhibiting violent tendencies. That sounds like the same patient we currently have down the hall. I mean, he just attacked Greta yesterday. I think you're reading into it too deeply, Sylvie. You're starting to see what you want to see."

Sylvie shot Dr. Lee a disheartened look as he closed the folder and handed it back to her.

"I mean, if you're *that* concerned about it," Dr. Lee continued, "you can always talk with Dr. Prichard on Thursday."

Sylvie nodded. "Thank you, Dr. Lee; I think I'll do that."

"Okay, well . . , I hate to leave you hanging like that, but I have a consultation with a surgeon at

Deacon Memorial in less than an hour. So, if you don't mind . . ,"

"Of course, doctor." She replied, hugging the file to her chest and stepping back to let him out of his office. "Thanks again."

"Anytime," he responded, walking away from her.

Sylvie watched the doctor disappear around the corner, then glanced down at the file she held in her hands. Her mind was made up; she knew what she needed to do. She told Dr. Lee she'd speak with Dr. Prichard on Thursday, but she had no intention of waiting that long. There was another who could supply the answers she sought. And, as it so happened, she had planned to meet with him anyway. Who better to know if Roger Loomis was the victim of experimentation than the man himself? Unless, of course, he had no idea what they were doing to him. All she had to do was ask. And then, as she always did, just listen.

Chapter 16

Observances

She never should have gone into the old file room, but now that she had, she couldn't let it go. Something troubled her about what she'd read in Roger's file. She'd made her mind up; Sylvie was determined to learn the answers.

Dr. Prichard was no longer on-site, so confronting him with her observations was no longer an option. She had another.

It wasn't exactly what she'd planned when she arrived earlier that morning; there were other matters she intended to discuss with her patient. Those thoughts seemed to slip from her mind in favor of learning about her latest discovery. Depending on what she ascertained, it could all be connected.

Sylvie marched down the corridor of patient bedrooms, the attendants diligently making their way from door to door, waking the patients for breakfast. Rounding the next corner and located halfway down the hall, there was one door that would remain closed, the one she was seeking, and outside that door, sitting in a small wooden chair, reading a book, was Tremont. He didn't notice Sylvie approaching until she spoke.

"Good Morning, Tremont. You're here early."

Peeling his eyes from his book and immediately standing, Tremont responded, "Yes, ma'am. I mean Miss Z. I've been coming in at three in the morning the past few days, covering for Josh – er, Mr. Ellison."

"Oh, is everything all right with Josh?"

"Oh yeah, he's fine," Tremont replied. "But since he started caring for his sick mother, he hasn't been getting much sleep. And I don't mind the overtime. In fact, I'm covering for Arturo tonight. He has to leave early; his daughter has a band recital at 8:30."

"Oh wow, that's a long shift."

"It's fine. It keeps my mind preoccupied, and the extra money helps with the medical bills."

Sylvie's eyes turned sympathetic as she reached up and gently rubbed the attendant's upper arm.

"And how *is* Aaron doing?" she asked.

Tremont tilted his head down, looking at the floor and nodding slightly. "He's good, good. He has his rough days, but he stays upbeat. He amazes me sometimes." Then he lifted his head, a more confident look on his face. "He's getting better; I can feel it."

"That's great, Tremont!" she said, smiling. "It's important to remain positive."

"And I did what you told me, Miss Z." he continued. "My wife and I spoke with Reverend Whiteley from our church. He gave us some encouraging words. I think everything is going to work out."

Sylvie gave Tremont a reassuring smile. "I hope it does."

Dropping her hand from his arm, she let the brief moment of silence permeate the hallway. It was a nice moment, she felt – one that would inevitably end when she continued.

"So, how is the patient this morning?" she questioned, changing the subject.

"He's been quiet," the large attendant answered. "Always reading."

"Well then, hopefully, that will make my job easier. Would you mind?" Sylvie pointed at the chair propped in front of the door.

"You sure you want to go in there?" Tremont questioned. "He doesn't usually like distractions this early in the morning."

Sylvie glanced through the door's window to find the patient lying face up on his bed, holding a book, his legs crossed at the ankles. He looked calm and relaxed – nothing like the file made him out to be. Nothing like she *knew* him to be.

"He'll get over this distraction," she stated.

"All right, Miss Z.," Tremont accepted, pulling the chair aside and allowing access to the door. "I'll keep watch over you."

Sylvie gave a slight smirk. "Thank you."

She opened the door and stepped inside. Roger had already sat up, having heard the chair scraping against the outside of the door. The book he'd been reading was open and placed upside down by his side to maintain his place. His hands rested on his lap, his fingers intertwined with each other. When he saw it was Sylvie, he slid his tongue slowly across his upper lip suggestively. Sylvie ignored the lewd gesture, marching directly to the desk, where she pulled its chair to the center of the room and sat down, facing her patient and placing the file on her lap.

"We meet again, Doctor," the man greeted her, his voice calm.

"Good Morning, Roger," Sylvie replied, her face displaying little emotion.

"Getting bolder, are we?" Roger questioned rhetorically. "A little bird told me you didn't like visiting me in my room."

"A little bird, huh?" she questioned, raising a single eyebrow at his remark. "You have no idea how bold I can be," she replied.

Roger supplied a devilish smirk, his eyes fixed on hers, "Oh, I think I have an inkling."

"Roger," she stated firmly to maintain control of the conversation, "I have some questions I'd like to ask you about your time at the Teton Psychiatric Hospital."

Roger's eyes shifted to the folder on the doctor's lap, the tab displaying a label with his name prominently marked in permanent ink. He smiled and raised his eyes back to hers.

"We've been over this, Doctor; we shouldn't dwell on the past. It holds . . , dark secrets."

"Funny you should say that, Roger," Sylvie responded, tilting her head slightly. "It's those 'dark secrets' I'd like to talk about. I'd appreciate your honesty."

The man, with his devious smile, nodded. "I've been nothing but honest with you from the start."

"Okay," Sylvie started, "how would you describe your stay at your previous location?"

Roger's smile suddenly faded. His eyes shifted to the folder again, then back up.

"What's in the folder?" he asked.

"I asked you a question, Roger," she stated uncompromisingly. "You said you've been honest with me. So, I'll ask again. How was your stay at Teton?"

Silence lingered for a few seconds before Roger replied.

"I think I like this new you — assertive, demanding, maybe even a little . . , domineering," he stated, giving her an insinuating wink. "Very well, Doctor. So, you want to know about my time at Teton? I had my good days and my bad days. And then I had my *very* bad days."

"Tell me about those very bad days," Sylvie insisted. "Why were they any worse than the others?"

Sylvie could see Roger's jaw tighten through his cheeks as he clenched his teeth.

"They said I was getting better," he replied. "I *wanted* to get better. Do you think I enjoyed the thoughts in my head? I was young and stupid. Why wouldn't I listen to the doctors? They promised me I'd change."

"And what were the doctors doing to help you?"

"Oh, you know, a little of this, a little of that."

"Can you be more specific?"

"I don't know that I can," he replied. "It all seemed so hush, hush. Perhaps I was being a little paranoid. I didn't know what was going on half the time. I felt like my mind was constantly in a fog."

"Did you feel like the doctors were helping you?" Sylvie asked.

"At first, yes. I didn't know any better. I was naïve. I thought all doctors wanted to help their patients."

"And later?"

Roger looked down at his hands. Sylvie noticed his thumbs had begun twitching. Without raising his head, Roger glared back at her, "Later, I knew better. Some only wish to help themselves."

Sylvie sat back in her chair, pondering her next question.

"Was Dr. Prichard one of the doctors 'helping you'?"

"Hmm . . , Dr. Prichard," he replied. "The name sounds familiar. Do I know him? I'm much better with faces, you know. I never forget a face."

Sylvie crossed her arms about her chest. "Will you quit with your bullshit, Roger?" she snapped in frustration. "Do you know about the medication the doctor was giving to you? Do you think Dr. Prichard was experimenting on you?"

"Doctor, everyone is always 'experimented' on. Nobody knows anything. We're all just a bunch of guinea pigs. Why all the questions, anyway? Did you perhaps learn something you'd care to share?"

Sylvie's eyes narrowed in response. She grabbed the folder from her lap and peeled back a few pages. Once she'd gotten to the section she was looking for, she turned it around and handed it to her not-so-cooperative patient.

"It states there, you were given an experimental drug on the morning of August 6th, 2003. You remember that date, don't you?"

"Ah yes, it always comes down to that date, doesn't it?" Roger answered. "The incident with that lovely, fresh-faced young woman was unfortunate."

"I *bet* you feel that way," she responded sarcastically. "But I'm not as concerned with the incident as much as I am with what took place beforehand."

"You didn't want to listen to what I had to say before," he griped.

"I listened," she replied. "But you didn't do yourself any favors with your cryptic comments. You said you were instructed to hurt that young intern. Was that what happened? Were you told to do that?"

"Would it matter if I was?" he questioned.

"It matters if it's true. Who told you to do it?"

"It's difficult to say," Roger replied, peering up at the ceiling. "I still hear the whispers, but the voice is unrecognizable."

"And what do the whispers say?"

Roger lowered his eyes, displaying an intense stare. "Not nice things. But then, the doctors tell me I'm schizophrenic or have schizoaffective disorder and that I'm paranoid, so what do I know? It's not like anyone will believe me, anyhow."

In between the seconds of silence, Sylvie stared into Roger's eyes to determine if he was speaking the truth. She wanted to believe him - she'd found documentation to support her theory – but psych patients didn't always know reality and truth.

"I think I'd like to change the subject," Sylvie said, gently pulling the folder back from Roger's hands.

"But we were making such progress, Doctor," Roger remarked.

Sylvie exhaled through her nose and smirked.

"Are you a violent man?"

Roger removed his hands from his lap and crossed them about his chest.

"Well, *that's* different," he stated. Roger's eyes swayed first to the ceiling and then to the side wall as he thought about it. Then they met hers. "I've never considered myself to be violent, no."

"Roger," she responded, tilting her head sideways and giving him an unbelieving stare, "you raped your foster sister, you beat and almost raped that intern, and you threatened Greta just yesterday."

"Ah, my foster sister. I try not to think about that time in my life. It can be woefully upsetting. The intern . . , well, as I stated, that was an unfortunate incident. We both know how that turned out. As for Greta, I mean, it was the handle of a plastic spoon. How much harm could I have done?"

"That's not exactly the point, Roger, now is it? But then, you told me it wasn't you holding the weapon. What did you mean by that? What happened after our meeting that morning?"

"Well, let's see. I remember you calling me disgusting."

Sylvie sneered. "And after that?"

"Let's just say I remember being me, but then, I wasn't."

"What do you mean?"

"I wish I could tell you, Doctor, but it's all a blur."

"Were you visited after our meeting?"

"I said, it's all a blur," he repeated. "Leave it be."

"I see," Sylvie responded. "One last thing, Roger. You warned me something was coming and that you couldn't stop it. What do you think is coming for me, Roger?"

"I never said it was coming for *you*. But don't worry, you'll know it when it happens."

Sylvie squinted and shook her head in confusion. She knew the interview was over; she was no longer getting anything useful from the man. The information she received from him wasn't as conclusive as she would have liked - but then, she wasn't expecting much. There was something strange going on; that much was obvious. And Dr. Prichard seemed to be in the middle of it. She had to be careful, however. It would be serious business to sling accusations without having all the facts. She'd need to gather more.

Exhaling heavily, Sylvie stood from the chair.

"Okay, Roger; I'll know it when it happens. Good talk. Let me know if you decide to fill me in on any of the gaps. I'm here to listen."

She turned for the door, not bothering to push the chair back under the desk. She'd let Roger handle that. As she reached for the knob, Roger called out to her.

"Oh, Doctor."

She turned her head.

"I'd be careful out there. In this place, we're all just puppets on strings. But what happens when those strings are severed? Watch yourself."

Sylvie shot Roger a perplexed glance. What was he going on about? It didn't matter. Finding out the truth about Dr. Prichard was foremost on her mind. That's what she needed to focus on. Thoughts of a mad scientist splashed across her brain.

She nodded and opened the door, leaving Tremont to close it behind her.

"Everything all right in there, Miss Z?" he asked.

She flashed him a smile. "It was . . , enlightening. I think I'm making progress."

Then she walked away, thinking of her next course of action.

Chapter 17

Disturbances

Throughout the day, Sylvie had a hard time remaining focused. She had sessions with six patients, all of whom deserved her full attention. Instead, she found herself having to ask the patients to repeat themselves since she'd been unable to focus on their initial responses. Her thoughts continued to wander back to her conversation with Roger Loomis.

When she sat with Alice Hodges, a woman with severe Bipolar Disorder, she asked the same question three times before realizing what she'd done. Sylvie never noticed the woman replied with a different response each time.

Harold Porch, another patient under her care, had a twenty-minute conversation with a sock puppet before Sylvie finally noticed, realizing that she had been staring over his head into the distance, allowing Harold to babble on – about what, she had no idea. From her baffled gaze, one would have thought she'd been intrigued by the two other patients playing checkers across the room, but, in truth, she never even saw them.

There was no excuse for her lack of attentiveness, only that her thoughts were preoccupied with the bewildering blatherings of a madman.

Was Roger a madman, she thought? *Or was there always more to his behavior than initially believed*? No. Medication aside, she knew the kind of monster he was. His past was a clear blueprint for who the man would always be. Whatever unusual treatment Roger might have sustained during his stay at Teton, it was more than likely deserved.

Even though she had such strong feelings, Sylvie managed to corral her thoughts long enough to type an email to the Psychiatric Administrator about her concerns but chose not to send it right away; she let it reside in her "draft" folder until she could discuss her findings with Dr. Prichard. Not to mention, bringing unwanted attention to herself was risky. If the administration began looking into Dr. Prichard's past, what would stop them from looking deeper into hers? That was something she couldn't allow. Not until she accomplished what she set out to do. Plus, would they even believe her? Or would they brush it aside and then target her for accusing a highly respected doctor and board member, regardless of whether they looked into her past?

Perhaps she was jumping to conclusions about what she'd read, anyway. After all, experimental drugs and trials on mental health patients were nothing new. Still, something didn't feel right - especially after some of the things Roger had stated. Then again, as a patient in a Psych hospital, Roger couldn't exactly be trusted. But she also knew she couldn't linger on the subject. She had a job to do and other patients to focus on.

Her shift was nearing its end as she exited her office into the constantly flickering hallway. She had one more patient to sit with, a simple follow-up session with Mr. Hoklin - a dear older man - before she could call it a day. As she locked her door, she again heard a scraping sound coming from the vacant office at the end of the hall, followed by a loud bang; she instantly jumped from her door, leaving her keys dangling from the lock.

"What the fuck?" she inadvertently screamed out, pressing her palm to her chest. She could feel her heartbeat thumping a mile a minute as she stared wide-eyed into the darkness at the end of the corridor.

"Who's down there?" she questioned.

Sylvie received no response as her eyes struggled to adjust between the strobing light above her head and the looming blackness in front of her. Her ears, however, were on high alert as she listened to every quivering breath entering and exiting her open mouth.

She had no idea what the strange noise could have been. She would have easily discarded the scraping noise as having come from a wandering mouse (she occasionally heard similar scraping noises from mice scurrying within the walls of her house) had it not been for the loud bang she'd heard. That didn't come from a mouse; someone was in the other office.

She'd been at her desk the past twenty-five minutes with the door open to the empty hallway; she would have seen or heard somebody pass by. If there was someone else down there, they had to have been there since before her arrival, yet she hadn't heard a peep until then.

"It's none of your business," Sylvie whispered to herself. It was all for nothing. Against her better judgment and with sheer stubbornness guiding her, she cautiously stepped toward the sound. "What does it matter?" she continued. "Just get upstairs where you're safe."

As much as she wanted to retreat, her feet wouldn't move in any other direction. It was like she was strolling in molasses against her will, unable to turn around no matter what she said to convince herself otherwise. "Why are you doing this? Grab your keys and hustle up the stairs where everyone else is - where the bad man can't get you."

Suddenly, fragmented comments from conversations she'd had with Roger echoed in her brain.

You need to get away from this place before it's too late. You can't stop what's coming.

Real nice, she thought. *Such encouraging words to think about while investigating mysterious noises in the dark. Maybe I should heed Roger's warnings and get away. Would it be so bad?* She shook her head at the idea.

That was just it, though; she was there for a reason. She couldn't pack up and leave until she finished what she had to do. She'd promised herself that much. And since she needed to remain until such time, she couldn't continue worrying about the strange noises coming from down the hall. She needed to confront them, or she'd slowly start going crazy – maybe even as crazy as some of her patients. That thought scared her more than the peculiar noises she'd heard, pressing her forward until she reached the far office's door.

Sylvie stared at the knob, momentarily numb and frozen in place while she listened for any movement. She heard nothing. Her hands were coiled in fists so tight her knuckles were turning white. Slowly, she brought one of those closed hands up by her shoulder, paused for a second, and then knocked on the door.

"Hello?" she called out.

The returned silence bothered her more than any response would have.

"Is there someone in there?"

Again, only silence.

Sylvie glanced to her right toward the stairwell to ensure she wouldn't again be startled by someone stealthily approaching. This time, she was alone. Shaking her head at her obstinance, she reached for the knob.

She couldn't believe what she was doing to satisfy her curiosity, but she was more fearful of not knowing. She needed to open the door to ease the anxiety she felt. She wasn't always as strong. She'd sheltered herself for many years after what had happened - after her parents .. , well .. , she wasn't always as strong. Maybe she thought she wasn't always as stupid, letting her thoughts turn everything into something it wasn't.

Gripping the knob tightly, she quickly swung the door open, half-expecting someone to charge at her. When nobody did, she felt a tingling sensation of relief crawl down her spine.

She also opened her eyes.

She flipped the light switch on the wall, listening for any scuttling a mouse might make running off in search of safety. There was nothing but the sound of her own breathing. As before, the office was empty.

She stepped inside to get a better look at things, this time peeking behind the door, a perfect hiding spot for someone ready to jump out and strike. There was nothing there but some dust and a crumpled ball of paper, no doubt a misfire meant for the waste basket when she had previously occupied that space. Basketball wasn't her sport. She spun around, scanning the small office for any evidence of skittering creatures that might have been there - droppings, nibbled chair cushions; there was no sign of any of it. She even walked behind the desk and bent over to look under it, even though she could clearly see from the front there was nothing and nobody underneath. Her old office was as it should be – lifeless and empty.

It's just your mind playing tricks on you again, she thought. *You've let your patients get inside your head. It's becoming too much. You've got to find a way to speed things up so you can get out of here.*

Sylvie let out a heavy breath, taking a last look around the office, then turned off the lights as she exited back into the gloomy hallway. The blackness seemed impossibly darker after having been in the lighted room. She quickly raced toward the brightened stairwell, snatching her hanging keys from her office door on her way by. She hated being down in the hospital's bowels. As if it wasn't creepy enough without the weird noises she'd been hearing.

As she ascended the staircase, Sylvie wondered what the noise could have been. Twice, she'd heard something coming from the vacant office. She knew it wasn't only in her head but, both times, she'd found nothing.

Wasn't that a good thing? she thought, emerging from the basement, oddly comforted by the surroundings of the hospital's main floor. She supposed it was, but it wouldn't stop her from nagging the maintenance crew into finally getting her some decent lighting (as if that would fix everything she was feeling).

With the uneasiness now behind her, Sylvie could finally calm down and focus on her therapy session with the sweet Mr. Hoklin. The man was such a bright spot in an otherwise dark place. He somehow always managed to find a way to make her feel better about the work she did. It was her last session before she could enjoy the weekend, and Sylvie couldn't have asked for a better patient with which to end her work week.

Piece of cake.

Chapter 18

Behavioral Issues

She had asked Mr. Hoklin how he felt about his granddaughter's last visit, and it all suddenly went to shit.

Moments earlier, Sylvie and the soft-spoken man were having a nice conversation about the beautiful weather they'd been having lately, the threatening storm notwithstanding. He always responded well to such exchanges. Mr. Hoklin loved all things nature. He'd often discuss different birds' nesting habits, which flowering plants attracted the most pollinators, and which local hiking trails offered the most beautiful views. Mr. Herbert Hoklin's fondest memories were of when he and his wife, Joseline, for whom he'd been married for forty-two years, would go on long nature walks together. He'd always spoken so lovingly of her. Because of that, it was a complete shock to learn he had come in from weeding their garden one morning and smothered her with his pillow while she lay napping in their bed.

Herbert had no recollection of murdering his beloved wife and was only made aware of it when his son stopped over that afternoon to find him lying beside the mother's dead body, the pillow still over her face, and an outlined impression of his father's dirty hand smudged in the center of it.

Sylvie regularly reminded Mr. Hoklin of the incident during therapy sessions, but he refused to believe he'd killed his wife or that she was even dead at all. He would often share stories about her periodic visits with him. Sylvie had a soft spot for the mild-tempered man, who would often talk about going home to his dear Joseline to discuss their plans for the future. They had planned a trip together and were only waiting for his release from the hospital. Sylvie couldn't break the news to him that he wasn't going to be released anytime soon, if ever.

Even after their numerous sessions, Sylvie never experienced an outburst or even uncooperative behavior from Herbert. That was, until that day.

It was a harmless question, one she often asked after a family member visited with a patient.

"How was the visit with your granddaughter, Mr. Hoklin?" Sylvie asked. *"It's Amelia, isn't it?"*

The kindly man smiled as if recalling the wonderful memory from the day before. He seemed as if he was about to express delight in the visit, but then his expression quickly soured. His eyes filled with rage, and his jaw clenched so tightly she thought he'd break his dentures. He began breathing so heavily through his mouth that bubbles of spit formed between the spaces of his teeth, spraying outwardly. His feet and legs began to twitch uncontrollably. Sylvie watched nervously and on edge as Mr. Hoklin's hands clenched the arms of his chair with such strength that he forced the blood from them.

Concerned, Sylvie leaned forward, "Mr. Hoklin, are you all right?"

Through clenched teeth, the elderly man responded, "Bitch! Bitch! Bitch!" as saliva dribbled from his lower lip onto his lap.

Without thinking, Sylvie slid forward in her chair and reached for his hand to calm him down. It was more out of reflex. As a trained psychologist, she knew better, but as a human being, she wanted to ease his pain. Mr. Hoklin instantly snatched his hand away and slapped her wrist.

"Ouch!" Sylvie cried, more startled by his reaction than she was physically hurt.

"Don't touch me, fucking bitch!" Mr. Hoklin seethed, spit spraying from his mouth.

"I think our session is over for today, Mr. Hoklin," Sylvie stated with noticeable concern (and slight irritation) as she glanced over his shoulder and waved her hand to alert the waiting attendant. "I think you need a little rest."

Mr. Hoklin immediately jumped up, pointing his finger at the doctor threateningly, causing Sylvie to kick her chair backward, almost tipping it over.

"Goddamn piece of shit whore!" he yelled, causing other patients from across the room to turn their gazes in the doctor's direction.

Sylvie sat frozen in her chair, wide-eyed, as the arriving attendant grabbed the older man's arm and forcefully yanked him away from their meeting area. She felt herself heavily swallow as she brought her trembling hand to her heaving chest, trying to gather herself.

As the attendant ushered Mr. Hoklin from the Day Room, the raving man lashed out, ripping the patients' shared phone from the wall beside the nurses' station and smashing it to the ground. The attendant quickly secured the man's limbs and hastily escorted him down the patient corridor.

What the hell was that? she thought, her eyes anxiously shifting in all directions. *I've never seen Mr. Hoklin act like that.*

While Sylvie sat there catching her breath, observing the other patients slowly returning to their activities, she noticed one of the staff nurses entering the assembly area from the patient rooms. She had with her a rolling medication cart. It wasn't something that would have normally caught Sylvie's attention, but with her nerves on edge and senses on full alert, she picked up on it right away.

It wasn't common practice to wheel medication into areas where the patients could gain access, even if in a locked cart. The cart's purpose was to transport drugs from the in-house pharmacy to the nurses' station, where patients would line up and wait for the medication to be distributed to them. They were on a strict schedule. Instinctively, she glanced at the clock on the far wall. It was almost 4:30, only a few hours after the patients' last scheduled rounds of medication. That was unusual and something she hadn't seen before, especially when the cart wasn't coming from the pharmacy.

She got up from her chair and scrambled over to the nurse, who was pushing the cart into the nurses' station.

"Nurse Sullivan," Sylvie announced, grabbing the nurse's attention as she approached.

"Yes, Dr. Zcieveteveicz?"

"I'm sorry, but I couldn't help but notice you had just come from the patients' rooms."

"Yes, that's right," the nurse replied.

"With the medication cart?" Sylvie pointed out, blatantly questioning the reasoning.

"Yes; is there a problem?"

Besides the obvious? Sylvie thought.

"Didn't the patients already receive their medication at 1:00?"

"Oh, yes, of course," Nurse Sullivan replied, smiling and nodding.

"Then what is this?" Sylvie inquired.

"Dr. Prichard is starting some patients on a new regimen."

"What do you mean? I wasn't made aware of this."

"Well, you don't make the decisions, Doctor Zcieveteveicz," Nurse Sullivan replied snidely. "And, frankly, you don't have to be informed. So, I don't know what to tell you."

"Well, you can start by telling me what you're giving them, and yes, I do need to be informed so I can carefully monitor and properly assist my patients."

Nurse Sullivan huffed. "It's a new supplemental drug Dr. Prichard ordered for clinical trials."

"What?" Sylvie questioned. "Dr. Prichard can't do clinical trials on patients without the proper consent."

"I'm afraid he can," Nurse Sullivan replied.

"What are you talking about?"

"Oh right, that was before you arrived here," the nurse stated with an unsympathetic look. "Many of the patients' family members offered their consent some time ago."

"This is unbelievable," Sylvie stated, raising her voice. "How many patients have you already given the drug to?"

"Only a small handful so far. Let's see . . , Hector, Sandra, Keith, Mr. Hoklin, Greta . . ,"

"Wait," Sylvie cut the nurse off. "Did you say Mr. Hoklin? That must be a mistake. Mr. Hoklin was just with me."

"Well, we knew Mr. Hoklin had his appointment with you at this time, so he was given his dose with his 1:00 medication. Dr. Prichard approved it."

"Oh, that's great," Sylvie responded sarcastically, "Dr. Prichard approved it. Wonderful. Do you even know what the drug is?"

"Yes, of course. It's Ditrolazipan Sulfate."

Sylvie shook her head, recognizing the name from Dr. Prichard's notes on Roger Loomis.

"What did you say?"

"I said it's Ditrolazipan Sulfate."

Suddenly, Sylvie felt a knot in the pit of her stomach. Dr. Prichard's notes indicated Roger had been given the same drug at Teton. He noted there were severe behavioral issues with the "subject." Mr. Hoklin displayed behavioral issues moments ago, something he'd never done during their sessions. Was it a side effect of the drug? She couldn't be sure, but it certainly seemed like a possibility.

"You have to stop," Sylvie stated. "You can't give them this drug."

"I'm sorry," the nurse responded, "but it's doctor's orders." She turned away from Sylvie and began pushing the cart forward.

Shaking her head at the nurse's response, Sylvie gently tugged at the woman's arm, turning her around once again.

"Excuse me," Sylvie said, annoyed, "but I'm a doctor too, and I said this has to stop."

Nurse Sullivan glanced down at Sylvie's hand still clutched around her arm, then offered a condescending smirk. "Yes, you're a doctor, Sylvie, but not one that can prescribe medication, are you? And certainly not the one in charge around here."

"What the fuck?" Sylvie remarked, dropping her hand from the nurse's arm. "What is wrong with you?"

"I told you," the nurse replied angrily, clenching her teeth, her eyes burning a hole in Sylvie, "doctor's orders."

Sylvie stood speechless, her mouth agape as she slowly shuffled backward.

"I can't let this go," Sylvie began. "I'm going to have to tell the Psychiatric Administrator about this." She turned and started walking toward the Day Room's exit when she heard the nurse's voice yell out.

"Who do you think approved it?"

Chapter 19

Let it Go

When Sylvie had exited the activities hall, she was determined to figure out what the hell was going on. But when she marched to her office to send out the email she'd saved, she began having second thoughts. It was Roger Loomis' glaring folder on her desk that caused her reluctance. She stood frozen, painfully staring at the file and struggling with what to do. She thought about the man he was, or, at least, the man she believed him to be. Mental disorder or not, he was detestable, a disgusting sex offender preying on the young. She knew she shouldn't think that way, but even as a psychologist, it was sometimes hard to separate her personal and professional feelings. And what of the later atrocities he'd committed while under psychiatric care? Now she wondered, was he even to blame?

Let it go, she thought.

What about the other patients who needed her help? She had a moral and professional obligation to each of them. If something unethical was going on at the hospital . . ,

Let it go.

Why should she even care? She was only at Somerset for one reason. If things worked out, she'd be gone soon enough. If she alerted the administration, things could get tricky. It could ruin everything.

Let it go, Sylvie.

And what of the smug Dr. Prichard? She thought. Would she be comfortable letting an arrogant ass like that get away with something unscrupulous if she had the power to bring him down? Would that, alone, be enough to satisfy her if the rest of her plan came crashing down? She already knew the answer.

You have to let it go. Those patients are not your problem. They're not yours to save.

While the two halves of her conscience battled for supremacy, she thought about her parents and how they had raised her to do what was right. Wasn't that what she was doing? Wasn't that why she chose this field?

Was it, though? Or was it something else?

Before she allowed her thoughts to answer that question, the power suddenly went out, leaving her in the dark and sending an immediate chill down her spine. She leaned against the desk to prevent herself from swaying and losing her balance. Her tiny space was so dark that she couldn't even see her hand in front of her face. Without warning, a strange clanging noise clamored from the wall to her right, causing her breathing to become shallower. Her anxious thoughts quickly rewound to an earlier time, a fearful, terror-stricken time when the "bad man" occupied her brain. It was as if he were there with her, breathing in her ear. The hair on her neck shot upward, reaching for the ceiling and pulling at her skin. Her heart was pounding so hard in her chest that she thought her ribs were about to break. Then, another frightening noise gripped her. A slowly building humming sound echoed from the walls around her, ripping into her very being before the lights instantly kicked back on.

At that saving moment, Sylvie felt her whole body relax as the entire weight of the room slid from her shoulders. Catching her breath and gaining strength in her wobbly legs, she gathered her things, scooped the folder from her desk, and quickly vacated her office, seeking higher ground. She sprinted up the staircase to the safety of the main floor. She didn't send the email; she didn't look back.

Sylvie had made up her mind. She always knew which way she'd lean, her conscience be damned. If it got her out of the hospital sooner — in more ways than one - she was willing to let it go. Whatever consequences the hospital faced after she was gone wasn't her problem. Finishing what she'd started was all that mattered.

When Sylvie reached the top of the stairs, an overwhelming sensation of relief enveloped her. But as she made her way to the sliding glass doors to leave the building, the lights suddenly flickered, and the power, once again, went out, leaving the entire floor in darkness save for the exit lights overhead, which glowed eerily against the walls and tile floor.

"Shit!" Sylvie blurted just as she heard Guarddog Glen yell, "Fuck!" from behind his closed door. The loss of power didn't seem as frightening on the main floor. The quickly fading daylight from outside cascaded through the vestibule doors, dimly lighting the area in front of the entryway. The glowing red exit signs, with their battery backup, were doing the rest of the job, providing enough light to guide Sylvie to the exit. It was pointless, however, as she quickly learned she wouldn't be leaving; she tried scanning her badge, but the exit doors wouldn't open.

Almost simultaneously, both Glen and Jules exited from their respective cubbies to join Sylvie in the hallway. Their doors, as with all of the office doors, were standard access, controlled by a lockset. The Day Room, elevators, and, of course, the main exit - the one door with which Sylvie was most concerned - were activated by electronic badge scanners.

"What the hell, guys?" Sylvie questioned, throwing her hands up and peering back and forth between the two.

"The news said there've been random power outages in some areas," Jules stated, remaining peppy, even in the dark.

"Isn't that what a generator is for?" Sylvie questioned.

"That goddamn thing?" Glen loudly announced. "It's on its last leg. I told them that piece of shit needed a stator replacement three years ago. Fuckers didn't want to listen to me then. Now they've got a company coming on Monday to replace the entire unit. The dimwits at the top could have saved themselves a boatload of money if they would have just listened to ol' Glenny-boy."

"Please tell me you have the override key," Sylvie said, peering at Glen with hopeful eyes. All the security guards had one, allowing them to override the scanners if need be, but Glen had forgotten his a few times, insisting on keeping it separate from his standard set for some unknown reason that only made sense to Glen.

"And did you just refer to yourself in the third person?" Sylvie questioned jokingly.

Glen shrugged his shoulders and smirked, "Hey, allow me this one moment, huh," he said, fumbling for the override key.

Then, just as before, a low rumbling was heard as the generator slowly kicked on, and the lights flickered to life.

"There we go," Glen offered, ending his search.

"Thank God," Sylvie responded. "Let me out of here."

She scanned her badge, opening the large doors.

"Have a good night, Sylvie," Jules stated, enthusiastically waving as Sylvie walked through the second set of doors.

"I will now," was Sylvie's response, her only thought being, *let it go, Sylvie. Just let it all go,* as she quickly walked to her vehicle.

Chapter 20

After Dark

The trough in the carpet was becoming more distinguished with each passing stride as Sylvie paced back and forth across her living room. She was having a hard time taking her own advice. She should have known better; letting things go was never her strong suit.

She was torn about what to do, pinching her lower lip between her forefinger and thumb as her thoughts wandered as aimlessly as her steps. Her eyes, too, drifted from side to side, unable to focus on anything except the occasional glance at the clock. Her most recent inspection of the time, which felt like an hour since her last glance, showed only three minutes had elapsed. Clearly, the situation at the hospital bothered her more than she cared to admit.

It wasn't like it should have mattered to her. She was only supposed to be a tourist, staying for a short time until the deed was done, in and out, quick and clean. But things got sticky. It didn't happen as she expected. She got to know the patients.

Had she not been so caught up with her own agenda, she might have noticed what was going on sooner.

Do I even know what's going on now? She thought.

Maybe she was jumping to conclusions. What was she so suspicious about? Dr. Prichard was a highly esteemed psychiatrist, praised by his colleagues, and a well-respected member of the Board. He'd spent years working with patients, trying to rehabilitate them - to get them reintegrated into society. He took the Hippocratic oath to never deliver harm to those under his care. She hadn't heard of any lawsuits filed against him, nor did she have a reason to believe there had ever been. She began thinking she was becoming paranoid simply because she had an agenda and nothing more.

She stopped pacing and glanced over at the folder sitting on her chair. It was funny how one little file could easily change one's perspective. She marched over and swiped it from the cushion, opening its cover to the pages within. Her pacing began anew, following the same worn path while she studied the words on the yellowing papers.

"In the matter of Mr. Loomis' condition - it is this doctor's professional opinion that the trials be started once again. The inconclusive nature of past subjects' results should not be a consideration for new and on-going treatment using the newly formulated Ditrol-26.

"The previous subjects were not, nor were they ever, ideal candidates due in part to the very nature of their deteriorating mental health. The women's disagreeable behaviors, for example, were most likely an unexpected side effect caused by their mental health disorders and not the administered drug.

"In conclusion, I believe further testing and evaluation of the current drug should continue until it produces favorable results and that preparations should be made for our latest subject, Mr. Loomis, to begin undergoing immediate specialized treatment."

Sylvie flipped the page, shaking her head and scanning the doctor's notes. She was shocked to learn how often Roger had been administered the experimental drug and how, with each dose, his temperament worsened. The doctor's annotations also indicated that Roger was becoming highly susceptible to suggestion, a notion that supported Roger's rantings during her discussion with him. He stated he heard whispering in his ear. The attack that took place at Teton, the incident that landed him in Somerset – he said he was "told" to do it. Sylvie looked up from the folder, trying to recall other things the man had said – to connect the pieces. Suddenly, her doorbell rang, causing her jerky hands to drop the folder onto the floor.

"Christ!" she yelled, looking down at the papers that had scattered in all directions. She thought of picking them up first, but a second ringing of the doorbell made her choice to answer the door more favorable. She hopped over the papers in her path and darted for the door before the annoying chimes could ring a third time.

It wasn't difficult to figure out who it was; nobody else ever visited her. So when she got to the door, she didn't bother looking through the shades to determine who her unexpected guest was.

"Come on in, Kevin," she announced, greeting the boy while opening the door.

The boy's face lit up with a smile as he entered.

"How'd you know it was me?" he questioned.

Sylvie narrowed her eyes and gave him a playful smirk, trying to look intimidating.

"You do know I'm psychic, right?" she answered, wiggling her fingers at him to appear more menacing.

"Yeah, right," he replied, laughing it off. Then, his face became serious. "Wait, are you?"

Sylvie rolled her eyes and giggled. "Nooo."

"Oh, okay," he responded, the smile returning as he took it upon himself to walk toward the living room. Before Sylvie could stop his advancement, he was already at the entryway, frozen at the edge of the carpet.

"What happened here?"

"Yeah," she replied, staring over his shoulder and scratching the back of her head, "that's what the doorbell did to me." She squeezed by her young guest to pick up the scattered mess.

"I thought you said if I used the doorbell, it wouldn't scare you."

"It didn't," she responded, blushing. "It was just . . , you know . . ." She looked up from her knees as she gathered some papers and noticed his unbelieving gaze. "Okay," she conceded, "maybe it scared me a little. You'll have to give me a second to pick this up since it was kinda your fault."

"Sure," the boy agreed.

As Sylvie shuffled her stack of papers together, she wasn't paying too much attention to the young boy until he commented.

"Isn't this the guy you told me about?" he inquired, plopped on his knees and staring at one of the pages he'd picked up. "The violent one? You said his name was Mr. Loomis."

"Hey!" Sylvie snapped, snatching the sheet from his fingers. "That's not for you to look at."

"Sorry, I didn't mean it. I was only trying to help. It was just there in front of me."

"It's okay, Kevin," she responded. "I didn't mean to snap at you. I can get the rest of this. Why don't you wait for me in the kitchen?"

The boy stood, demonstrating his unhappiness with his slow rise. Sylvie picked up on it right away and offered an encouraging smile.

"Thank you so much for the help, Kevin. I'll be right out."

The boy nodded and quickly dashed from the room. She listened for the familiar sound of the kitchen chair scraping across the tile floor before she continued heaping the stack of papers back into the folder. A minute later, when she was through, she stepped into the kitchen, leaving the file on the couch cushion.

"So, what's going on, kiddo?" Sylvie questioned, pulling out the chair across from the boy.

"Nothin'. I was just bored."

"Yeah, I get that way sometimes, too."

Then, silence took over the conversation as Kevin's eyes shifted downward to the table. Sylvie decided to jump right back in.

"You still feeling upset about your parents arguing?"

The boy looked up at her, his appearance optimistic. "Actually, I talked with my mom about it. She said there was no chance she and my dad were getting divorced. I don't know; she said something about my dad making too much money for her to ever leave him, and he was too needy to make it on his own. Whatever that means."

Sylvie raised her hand in front of her mouth and cleared her throat to keep from giggling.

"I see," she replied, holding back a smile. "Well, that's . . , good news."

"Yeah, I guess." Then, as if feeling guilty about something, Kevin turned his head away from Sylvie. "I'm sorry about what happened in the living room."

"Oh, hey," Sylvie responded, reaching forward and cupping her hand over his, "it's fine. Really. It wasn't as big a deal as I made it seem."

"Is that your only patient?" he asked.

"No," she smiled, pulling her hand away. "I have many."

"Girls too?"

"Yes, I have some women patients, as well."

"Are they as messed up as that guy?"

Sylvie shot the boy a stern glare. "I think you know that's not appropriate to say."

"Sorry."

"But to answer your question, some of the women do have severe psychological disor . . ," She stopped in mid-sentence and stared over the boy's head, her thoughts latching onto something.

"Are you okay, Sylvie?"

Her eyes shifted back to his. "Oh, um . . , yeah. You know what, Kevin," she said, jumping up from her chair, "I think I'm going to have to ask you to leave."

"Was it something I said?" he questioned.

"Oh, honey, I didn't mean it like that. But yes, it was something you said. In a good way. You reminded me of something I have to check on."

"At the hospital?" Kevin inquired.

"Yes, I think I forgot something. I'm going to need you to skedaddle, young man."

Kevin pushed himself up and shuffled to the door.

"You've been a tremendous help, Kevin. I mean it. More than you know."

He turned and faked a smile. "Glad I could help, Sylvie." Then he walked out the door.

Sylvie felt her heart drop. Kevin was such a sweet boy; the last thing she wanted to do was hurt his feelings. But she couldn't worry about that now. The boy *did* help her. Well, possibly. She'd know soon enough. She quickly grabbed her jacket, which was flopped over the arm of the couch, and raced back to the kitchen door. It wasn't what she'd planned for the start of her weekend; she hadn't even had dinner yet. It was 7:00 on a Friday night, but she was heading back to Somerset.

Chapter 21

The List

"How's it going tonight, Arturo?" Sylvie asked the second-shift psychiatric attendant through her open window as he pulled alongside her on his way out of the entrance.

"It's as quiet as it ever is, Doctor. What brings you here at this hour?"

"You know, I can't seem to get enough of this place," she replied.

"If that were true, maybe *you* should be the one committed."

Sylvie forced a smile, knowing his remark was meant only in jest. "I forgot some files. I wanted to get some research done before next week."

"You *must* be crazy for wanting to work over the weekend."

"I guess I've come to the right place then," she responded, offering him a quick wink, showing her lighter side.

"Suit yourself," Arturo replied. "I've got to get going, though."

"Yes, I heard. Wish your daughter good luck tonight for me."

"Will do," he said as Sylvie pulled past him, watching in her side mirror as Arturo shook his arm out the window in a wave.

It was a lonely drive from the road's entrance to the staff parking lot - about a quarter of a mile. The hospital, built in the late forties, was set way back from the road, far enough away from curious gawkers who might otherwise take notice of the horrible conditions to which the patients of that era were subjected. The hospital's grounds were quite large and very lovely to view during the lighted hours, with its perfectly manicured, lush green lawns and magnificently groomed flower gardens blossoming with life, a panoramic splendor of beauty disguising the dark practices that once took place within its cold walls.

Although much had changed with patient care since that time, as well as updates and expansion to the building itself, the surrounding landscape remained unchanged, a sight that often put Sylvie's mind at ease on the morning drive in. But at night, with looming storm clouds gathering overhead, everything seemed so gloomy, and her mind was anything but at ease.

She wondered why she took such an interest. She cared for her patients (most of them, anyway), but nothing in Teton's or Somerset's past would change the fact that she would soon be gone, leaving it all behind her. But this wasn't the past or the future; this was the present, and as long as she remained at Somerset, her patients' mental well-being was under her careful watch. If the patients were wrongly prescribed medication that negatively affected them, hindering methods of treatment toward their possible recovery, she needed to intervene.

Sylvie needed to understand more about the drug being administered to the patients and why. During her limited research, she couldn't find anything about Ditrolazipan Sulfate, not a single mention of it on any of the medical or pharmaceutical sites she'd visited, including the FDA's searchable database. She wasn't at all surprised. Many trial and experimental medications weren't available to the general public. But, since she couldn't research the drug itself, she could at least research the effects it had on past and current patients.

She parked in her usual spot, several rows from the building's side face, even though spaces were available closer to the walkway. She grabbed her badge from the passenger side floor, where it had fallen during the short drive, and opened her driver's side door.

The night, though dark and threatening of rain, was exceptionally calm and in great contrast to the tumultuous nature of her sporadic thoughts as she stepped from her vehicle. She couldn't help but notice how bleak the facility's exterior looked under the cloud-covered moon and imagined many of the hospital's long-standing residents having similar thoughts about the building's *interior*. Or maybe some of them just felt they had depressing lives.

Sylvie hastily walked to the front entrance, expecting to see Venessa buried nose-deep in a book again. The off-shift security detail wasn't the most exciting of jobs, but one that seemed to suit Venessa just fine. Instead, to Sylvie's surprise, the brightly lit vestibule was empty. She shrugged her shoulders and scanned herself in, somewhat disappointed that she wouldn't be greeted by Venessa's oft-times playfully inappropriate comments. Striding past the empty guard window, she hoped she had better success with her badge on the inside scanner than earlier that morning. She didn't feel like banging on the glass until someone eventually came running to buzz her in. Thankfully, the light turned green, allowing her access.

She took a sharp left into the narrow hallway, heading straight for the stairwell to the basement - her least favorite area. She figured she'd start in the old file room before disrupting some of the patients' nightly routines. She still had a little time before they were shuffled off to their rooms for the evening.

When she reached the top step, she immediately noticed the constant illumination of the lower level with no interruption in the light's fluorescent glow. Her first thought was that Dr. Prichard had notified maintenance before he left that morning, as he mentioned he would. By the time she reached the fifth step, however, the light began blinking incessantly as it always had, dashing her hopes for reduced anxiety.

Once in the basement, Sylvie's focus remained straight ahead on the old file room door, choosing not to look in the direction of her office down the darkened left corridor. It would only serve to heighten her already increased level of apprehension and unease.

Scanning her badge at the door, she entered the tiny room filled with dated filing cabinets; the motion-activated light flashed to life.

At least the light in here works as it should, she thought.

Wasting no time, she jumped right to the cabinet she'd pulled Roger's file from, hoping to find other patients from that timeframe who were also experimented on.

Is that even the right word, she wondered?

"Experimented" sounded so dirty. The patient or their guardian could have consented to the clinical trials. For all she knew, everything was entirely by the book.

Pulling the drawer open and flipping through the files, Sylvie's thoughts jumped to earlier that afternoon when Mr. Hoklin's behavior suddenly turned rabid. She'd never seen him act in such a way, thinking him incapable of such intense anger.

He killed his wife, she thought. *Of course, he's capable.*

Still, his personality seemed to change instantly and without provocation. Was it only a coincidence he'd taken the Ditrolazipan Sulfate earlier in the day? Was there something in its composition that sparked a chemical change within the man's brain? Dr. Prichard's notes on Roger Loomis indicated similar results, but that was twenty years earlier. If the trials had continued back then, Roger's worsening behavior should have necessitated a change to the drug's chemical makeup, which would have yielded better results with reduced side effects. Dr. Prichard's own notes from 2002 stated such.

"...further testing and evaluation of the current drug should continue until it produces favorable results..."

Sylvie wasn't getting anywhere ruffling through the patient files. She couldn't find any other references to the mysterious drug or anything about continued trials taking place. Frustrated, she slammed the drawer closed, causing the two drawers below it to pop open.

What are you doing, Sylvie, she thought, pausing for a moment. She took a deep breath, staring at the open drawer and rubbing her forehead to calm herself. *It's all so ridiculous*, she thought. *You don't owe these people anything. You don't owe Roger Loomis anything.*

Shaking her head and displaying a disappointed grin, Sylvie calmly pushed the first drawer closed. When she went to do the same to the bottom drawer, the printed words on the singular folder within sent a chill down her spine.

Slowly, nervously, she pulled the manila file from its outer hanging folder, the words "Ditrol-26 subjects" labeled on its tab. It was what she was looking for, but the file was so thin. She opened it to find its entire contents was only a single piece of paper with the words "Discontinuation of Ditrolazipan Sulfate due to adverse results in test subjects" printed at the top in bold letters. The document was dated April 13, 2007. On the rest of the paper was a list of names and dates, in no discernable order, of the patients who'd been administered the experimental drug. Her eyes quickly skimmed the names.

Harold Ventile	2004
Peter Westlake	2007
Sophia Ranch	2004
Roger Loomis	2001
Claudia Frye	2005
Marcus Hoyte	2006
Eve Depo-Jenkins	2004

The list went on down the page – twenty-three names in all. At the bottom, the last four names were missing, torn from the sheet, leaving only the dates 2006, 2002, 2002, and 2003 visible. It didn't matter; the paper was only a list of names, of whom only one she recognized. But something didn't make sense. If she were to believe the document's heading, and she had no reason not to, Ditrolazipan Sulfate had been discontinued in 2007. If that were true, how were the patients being administered that same drug earlier in the day? Either way, a single paper with a list of names didn't get her any closer to learning the truth. Frustrated, she dropped the useless folder back into the drawer.

Then, without warning, as if her anxiety hadn't already reached its limit, the power went out.

"Great, just what I needed," Sylvie spoke aloud.

Chapter 22

The Silence

Sylvie stood in the darkness, unmoving, trying desperately to keep from hyperventilating. She wanted to fall to her knees but couldn't get her legs to respond to her brain's silent command. A minute seemed like an hour as she felt the darkness slowly suffocating her, gripping her in its unrelenting choke-hold and stealing the very breath from her lungs. Somehow, it felt alive, physical, brushing against her, causing her body to sway. She knew it wasn't possible, that her mind was playing tricks on her, but the experience felt too real to ignore.

"Fuck! Shit!" she cried out, mostly to know that she still had a voice should she need it. She felt a droplet of sweat drip down her forehead, matching the bead she felt under her blouse,

188

crawling down her side from her armpit until it mingled with her bra.

Get a hold of yourself, Sylvie, she thought. *Christ, you've endured worse than this. It's only another blackout like before. Pull yourself together, and get the fuck out of here.*

She blindly fumbled for the door, scraping the back of her right hand against the corner of a filing cabinet, tearing the skin clean off and leaving a gash. It hardly registered; her thoughts were on escaping the room. She'd feel the throbbing pain later. Catching the door's handle on her second swipe, she yanked the door open, pinching her fingers between the handle and the same troublesome cabinet now decorated with a layer of her skin. *That* pain she felt as she let out a sharp yell.

"Ouch! Goddammit!"

She shook her hand, trying to dull the pain as she exited into the dark hallway, not realizing she was sending droplets of blood scattering in all directions. She assumed the liquid she felt was the same sweat she felt everywhere else.

Looking toward the stairs, she could hardly see the faint outline of the treads, the softened red glow of the lit exit signs from the hallway above barely penetrating the stairwell's engulfing darkness. It wasn't much, but it was something, and she was grateful for it.

Stepping with renewed vigor, Sylvie hastened her pace the short distance to the staircase, grabbed the railing for balance, and heavily trodded up to the main floor. She hoped to join with others who were equally concerned with the frequency at which the power outages were happening.

How long will it be this time before the generator kicks on, she thought? *If at all?* It had already felt like hours.

As if tuned to her thoughts, when she reached the top step, a loud squealing sound was heard – like a slipping drive belt under the hood of a vehicle – and the power kicked on.

The weight of the moment suddenly melted away, leaving her to wonder why she'd insisted on going to the hospital in the first place. She told herself she needed to stop caring as much instead of catering to her sympathetic tendencies. She knew why she did it. There was just something about the entire situation – Roger's strange comments, Dr. Prichard's time at Teton, the documents she'd discovered, Mr. Hoklin's sudden erratic behavior – it gnawed at her gut. Now that she'd had her moment of angst, however, feeling trapped in the blackened pit of the hospital, none of it seemed as important as getting away. The sliding glass doors were just up ahead, inviting her to abandon any logical reason for staying. Who was she to turn down such a considerate invitation?

She pulled her badge from her left pocket as she approached the vestibule doors, noticing how quiet everything seemed. She half-expected the main corridor to be teeming with other frustrated hospital personnel. Instead, it was numbing silence that occupied the main floor. She flashed her badge in front of the door's electronic scanner and watched in discontentment as the red light stayed red.

"Shit, shit, not again; this isn't happening," she said in frustration, waving her badge several times at the face of the malfunctioning unit. Sylvie glanced through the large glass panes into the vestibule's waiting area, cupping her hands between her forehead and the glass to suppress the glare from the overhead lights. She hoped to find Venessa posted back at her station in the little hole in the wall. She wasn't. Instead, Sylvie felt something drip onto her cheek. She quickly pulled away from the glass, instinctively looking up for a leak in the ceiling before noticing the back of her hand was covered in blood. That was when the burning sensation set in.

"Fuck!" she exclaimed, wiping her cheek of the liquid and looking at the red smear on her fingers to confirm it was her blood that dripped on her. She tucked her badge away in her shirt's breast pocket and pressed her opposite palm against the back of her bloodied hand, hoping to quell the sudden throbbing coming from the open wound. It wasn't working.

Sylvie looked down the hallway to her left, where the bathrooms were only a short distance from her, just beyond the locked steel door. She wasn't holding out much hope of gaining access. It had the same electronic scanner as the entrance. She decided to try anyway; what else was she to do? She wasn't going back downstairs to use *that* bathroom. Not if she could help it.

She quickly marched to the cold, metal door, pulling out her badge from her shirt pocket, the scanner's red light taunting her. She gave it a quick swipe, and the light turned green, followed by a clicking sound that offered soothing relief to her growing anxiety. She still had a ways to go before she would feel better about the situation, but it was a start.

She tugged at the heavy door and entered the intermediate space where the doctors' offices resided between the main corridor and the patient activities area. Taking a glance down the left hallway toward the offices, she hoped to find the night nurse wandering about. She wasn't picky, though. She'd even settle for a stray attendant leaving the break room. She didn't want to be alone and could use someone to hear her complaints about the non-working entryway scanner. But instead, it was quiet. Unusually so.

Being so used to working the morning shift, Sylvie wasn't familiar with such silence. She never considered it could be as quiet as it was during the later hours.

She brushed it off and entered the first bathroom door on her right. She'd already noticed the pain in her hand slowly subsiding, but it was a pretty good gouge she had, and the blood hadn't yet stopped. She realized how she must have gotten the wound and imagined the next person going into the basement file room, finding a shriveled layer of skin hanging from the corner of the filing cabinet.

Better them than me, she thought, curling up the corner of her lip at the very idea of it.

She ran the cold water over her bloody hand, wincing as streams of blood splashed into the porcelain sink, spraying errant droplets of pink against its side walls. She rested her arms against the front rim, letting the water wash away the last of the pain and trickling plasma. She looked at herself in the mirror, shaking her head at the person looking back.

If only it were as easy to wash away the past, she thought. *Would I even be here to look after the patients?* Then, from her straying thoughts, it dawned on her.

It hadn't immediately occurred to Sylvie, with her thoughts more focused on her aching hand, but now that she'd had a moment of calmness, she couldn't wipe it from her mind. When she first entered the office area just outside the bathrooms, she had a clear view ahead of her into the Day Room through the large glass door, yet she didn't recall seeing a single patient. It was strange she hadn't immediately noticed. It had always been a comforting sight to her whenever she walked in.

Turning the faucet off, Sylvie grabbed a paper towel from the dispenser and lightly dabbed the back of her hand dry, feeling the sting of each touch before grabbing a second one to wrap around her wound. The blood had stopped, leaving the sticky layer under the epidermis exposed. The last thing she needed, on top of all her other problems, was to get an infection. With her luck, which only ever seemed to be horrible, doctors would need to amputate her arm at the shoulder to keep it from spreading.

No, thank you, she thought.

Wrapping the rough paper over the gash and pulling the two ends of the towel into her palm to hold tight within her fist, she exited the bathroom into the hallway. The corridor straight ahead, housing the three doctors' offices, with their lights off and doors closed, was still vacant. Sylvie looked to her right, peering through the glass door into the empty assembly area. Everything was so still and quiet. Even the soft, relaxing elevator music that continuously played from the overhead speakers fought hard to overcome the overwhelming silence.

Sylvie walked back to the steel door and peeked through the reinforced security glass window into the main hallway to see if there was any activity. There wasn't.

What the hell is going on here, she thought. *Where is everybody?*

She turned back to the activities hall and peered in through the door's glass pane, noticing the clock on the wall, its hands displaying a time of 8:07.

Why are there no patients? She wondered.

Shutdown for the night wasn't for another hour, where patients were hurriedly shuffled off to their rooms to enjoy some quiet time. Sylvie never agreed with the hospital's practice of early evening retirement but understood the reasoning. The hospital had such limited staff during the nighttime hours. Although, at the moment, the staff seemed to have dwindled from limited to non-existent. Sylvie wondered if that could be it. Perhaps there was a disturbance in one of the patients' rooms, drawing everyone, including Venessa, to the scene. It certainly wouldn't be the first time a patient had a hysterical outburst.

That can't be it, Sylvie thought. *There'd still be others around.* If nothing else, she was succeeding at working herself up.

Regardless of what was going on, she needed to find someone, anyone, if only to have them let her out of the building. She had no plans of staying the weekend. Venessa was her best bet since she would have a manual override key for the front doors. Sylvie waved her badge at the Day Room's scanner, watched the light turn green, and stepped into the quiet space. It was an eerie feeling, the room being so empty. She imagined what it must be like for those on the overnight shift, working in a place so devoid of life during the nighttime hours. Though it wasn't a pleasant thought, that wasn't her concern. She just wanted to find someone to know she wasn't alone.

Get your act together, Sylvie thought, shrugging off the bitter feeling that tugged at her a second before. *Find someone and get out of here.*

And with that thought, she headed toward the back hallway leading to the patients' rooms.

Chapter 23

Panic in the Halls

Sylvie scampered past the deserted nurses' station on her way to the rear corridor, glimpsing the untidy desk through the thick, polycarbonate window. She continued past the rear locked entrance of the doctors' offices and landed at the foot of the narrow hallway leading to the patient rooms. She stopped to listen for any commotion that might be taking place around the corner, thinking it wise if she first ensured it was safe for her to travel the winding halls alone. Then again, she wasn't given much choice.

"Hello?" she called out, hoping for a response. When none came, Sylvie drew in a heavy breath and sighed. The continued silence was discouraging, if not a bit disturbing. The abandoned hallway, adorned with framed canvas paintings of dated landscapes from a bygone era, opened its cold, empty arms to her. Nothing about it was inviting, however, only serving to remind her of another time, another life - one she never wished to revisit. With each passing second, she became more aware of how alone she was, her nerves flaring and reaching their breaking point.

At the far end of the corridor, where a locked door marked the entrance to the infirmary - Dr. Lee's territory - the hallway took a sharp right to the first set of patient quarters. As she slowly made her way to the end of the hall, Sylvie was relieved to hear faint mumblings coming from the patient rooms. That was one mystery solved. Now, if only she could locate a staff member.

She walked down the second hallway that led to an intersection at the end, stopping at each room along the way to peek into each door's small window to see if a nurse or attendant was present. They weren't, but she did learn most of the noise she'd heard was coming from Joseph Stanley's room as he swayed back and forth, dancing by himself in the center of his room, humming a tune from the late '90s. He probably thought he was dancing with his ex-wife, whom he'd never gotten over, even after she remarried. It's also probably why he killed the new husband after running into him in a hardware store, smashing his head several times with a claw hammer. Joseph's attorney argued that his client's actions were a crime of passion, hoping to minimize his prison stay. The jury didn't buy it, finding him guilty of second-degree murder. The judge was lenient, however, noting Joseph's peculiar behavior during the trial. At the behest of both attorneys, he ordered that Joseph undergo a complete psychiatric evaluation, to which he was deemed mentally unstable. He probably belonged in prison but was sentenced to a stay at Somerset instead, where he could be closely monitored and evaluated. Although, watching him through the window, it appeared the years spent within Somerset had slowly driven him more insane.

When Sylvie arrived at the intersection, she first glanced right. There was nothing but an empty hallway lined with closed doors. She then looked to her left, and in a split second, all the fear she thought she'd suppressed suddenly crashed into her like a battering ram.

Halfway down the hall, Tremont lay on the floor outside Roger Loomis' room, his body motionless, and Roger's door swung open. Repressing her first instinct, which was to run away, Sylvie ran toward Tremont to check on him.

"Tremont!" she yelled, arriving at his unmoving body. He was breathing but unconscious and had a large gash on his forehead that needed medical attention.

"Tremont," she cried again, shaking his arm to see if he'd awake. "Tremont. Shit, shit."

She leaned forward and peeked inside Roger's room; he was gone. She looked ahead of her and screamed, "Help! Somebody help me." It was no use. She looked behind her, thinking of what she needed to do. If she couldn't find a nurse, she needed to call 911. She looked back at the unconscious attendant, rubbing his arm. "I've got to go find help, Tremont," she stated, unaware if he could hear her. "I need you to hang in there. I'll be right back."

She jumped up and sprinted back down the hallway. She hated leaving Tremont like that, but there was nothing else she could do. She had no idea of the severity of his injuries. She needed to get to a phone.

You're the only person I know who doesn't have a cell phone.

Kevin's words clambered in her head louder than they ever had before.

You're the only person . . ,

"Shut up!" Sylvie let out, silencing the voice. "I get it."

Back in the large assembly room, she couldn't help glancing at the vacant spot on the wall where the patients' shared phone used to be before the raging Mr. Hoklin got his mitts on it.

That would have come in handy right now, she thought. Shaking it off, she quickly scanned her badge at the rear door into the doctors' offices. Her thoughts still reeling, she ran to Dr. Prichard's office and rattled the doorknob.

"Fuck!" she exclaimed, now more concerned for the attendant she'd left behind. Dr. Lee's office was next - also locked. The nurse's station, too, was closed up tight, as was the vacationing Dr. Bingham's office.

"Come on, come on. Shit! Think, Sylvie. Maybe Venessa is back."

She ran around the front corner to the steel door, fumbled for her badge, and scanned the door open. Just as she entered the main hallway, the lights went out, causing Sylvie to halt her progression.

"Fuck you!" She yelled, looking up at the glowing exit signs with annoyance. It was silly, she knew, but it felt good to let it out. Tucking her badge into her pants pocket, she continued running toward the security station.

Just past the entrance vestibule, as Sylvie reached the guard's door, her foot slipped out from under her, and she fell onto her side. She pushed herself to a seated position and immediately felt the liquid under her hands.

"What the fuck?" she questioned, looking at her hands and seeing enough from the overhead glow to notice the makeshift paper towel bandage drenched in red.

"What the fuck? What the fuck?" she mumbled, looking down and noticing her legs were sitting in a puddle of blood, her hands dripping with the liquid. Her heart began pounding through her chest.

Grabbing onto the security guard's doorknob to pull herself up, her hand slick and struggling to maintain a grip, Sylvie somehow managed to make it to her feet. Just as she did, a rumbling sound signaled the generator coming to life, and the lights kicked on.

"Thank God," she said, hunched over and looking down at her blood-stained clothes. That was when she noticed the blood had leaked from under the guard's door. Her eyes wide and her heart racing, she slowly stood up, fearful of what she'd see. Peering into the security office through the door's small window, Sylvie felt herself become light-headed.

"No, no, no, no. Venessa!"

Venessa was sitting on the floor, her body slumped against her chair, her neck spewing blood. Most of it had seeped into her uniform, but a small stream had trickled beyond the woman's feet and pooled outside the security office door. Sylvie frantically wriggled the doorknob, trying to gain entry. It was no use. The door had been locked, most likely by whoever had done that to the woman. She dry-heaved, trying to hold down her dinner as she bent over, pressing her trembling palms against her knees for stability. As she stood there catching her breath, her stomach in knots, her stare shifted to the blood-soaked paper towel on her hand, and her thoughts strangely jumped to the possibility of communicable diseases. All hospital staff members were required to get tested yearly, but a lot could have happened in a year. Under the circumstances, it was probably more hysteria setting in than worry.

"Shit."

She slowly pulled at the bandage, wincing from the paper fibers sticking to the wound until it was finally free. Dropping the dripping towel to the floor, she shook her hand to alleviate the stinging before gently wiping it across her thigh. Shaking her head in disbelief that something as awful as this could be happening, she stepped toward the front door to try its scanner again. If she could get outside, she could drive to the nearest store or gas station and alert someone of the situation. They'd call the authorities and get the whole thing straightened out, and more importantly, she'd be safe.

Even with the thunderous pounding of her heartbeat exploding between her ears, a clicking sound suddenly gained her attention. It was the gray, metal door down the hall unlocking. Somebody swiped their badge; she wasn't alone in this. A feeling of incredible relief washed over her, sending a tingling sensation down her spine as she closed her eyes and let out a heavy breath.

Oh, thank God, she thought.

She rubbed the back of her uninjured hand across her brow, feeling the soothing dampness of its sweat. It reminded her of the warm, wet facecloth her mother used to drape over her forehead when, as a little girl, she felt sick, though it didn't compare to the sickness she was feeling at the moment.

As the heavy steel door began to swing open, her salvation only a short distance away, slowly, Sylvie opened her eyes.

Chapter 24

You've Been Hiding

Timing, as they say, is everything – never more true than when telling a good joke. You have to keep the audience captivated and wanting more. That's what this was, all just a big joke. The universe was playing a joke on her. But Sylvie didn't want more. She'd had enough. She was ready for it to end. The universe, however, had other plans. And timing, as they say, is everything.

As Sylvie slowly opened her eyes to the sound of the steel door swinging open, the cruel hand of fate took over, and the low humming sound that offered light from above in these darkest moments waned. The overhead fluorescents flickered rhythmically to the generator's random sputtering, until eventually, the lights faded, and everything went black. The dim exit signs flashed on and did their best to light the hall, but only enough for Sylvie to make out the shadowy silhouette of her would-be savior. It was the voice, however - *his* voice - that grabbed her insides and squeezed.

"I told you to get out of here while you could," the harsh voice said. "But you didn't want to listen."

Sylvie's blood ran cold. She slowly backed away, clinging to the wall, her breath becoming shallower with every step as the metal door behind the man's threatening outline clanged shut.

"Roger, what did you do?" Sylvie asked calmly, trying not to give away her fear.

She watched as the darkened figure slowly stepped forward, his pace matching hers, every step causing her heart to thump harder within her chest.

"What did *I* do?" he questioned angrily. "What did *I* do? What did *you* do? You couldn't leave well enough alone. Now look at the mess you've caused."

Continuing to back up, leaving a trail of bloody footsteps in her wake, Sylvie felt herself begin to tremble. Besides Tremont, who, for all she knew, was lying dead in the hallway, she hadn't seen another attendant or nurse around. Even if they were right beyond the steel door, they were now locked away, unable to help her. She was alone and defenseless, trapped with an unbalanced man.

Young Kevin's words snapped into her head.

Is he dangerous?

To which she replied, *He has the potential to be dangerous, yes.*

It was always in her brain. She hadn't seen it during her time at Somerset, but she knew what Roger Loomis was capable of. Of all her grand scheming when she signed on to be Somerset's resident psychologist, this was never part of the plan. And now, it seemed she might never get the opportunity to accomplish what she'd set out to do. Her only chance to get out alive was to try and reason with an unreasonable man.

"Roger, listen to me," she said, still retreating. "It doesn't have to be this way. I know what they did to you; it wasn't your fault."

"My fault?" Roger seethed, spit flying from his lips. "You think I wanted any of this? You've got it all wrong. But you're going to learn. Do you hear me? Are you listening now? You're going to learn."

Roger began walking faster in her direction, the glow of the red lights splashing across his face as he passed under them, making his features look like a crazed lunatic. His bushy eyebrows furled angrily over his narrowed stare, his nose was scrunched, and his lips were peeled open in a snarl, bearing teeth like a rabid Doberman ready to pounce. He was only a man, of course, but under the red lights, he looked like the devil himself.

Sylvie glimpsed the staircase to the basement on her left and darted for them. All she could think about was getting to her office to call for help. She could barely see the stairs as she descended, her legs moving as fast as they could. It wasn't the smartest thing to do, sprinting with wet shoes on the wooden treads, something she quickly learned when her feet slipped out from under her, and she tumbled backward, slamming her back into the stairs and sliding the remaining steps to the floor. On a positive note, it certainly was the faster route, albeit more painful, as she agonizingly pushed herself to her feet. Had the rush of adrenaline not been pumping rampantly through her body, she would have remained on the ground a while longer, unable to move.

Pressing her left hand against her throbbing lower back, Sylvie hobbled toward her office, peering back up the stairs. Roger hadn't yet gotten there. If she could get to her phone and dial 911, she could lock herself in her office and wait for the authorities to arrive. She dug into her pocket to retrieve her keys, the back of her injured hand scraping against the rough fabric, causing her body to stiffen up from the pain. She pressed on, feeling for the doorknob with her left hand while she yanked the keys free from her pocket. She let out a sharp yell.

"Ouch! Fuck!"

Sylvie had only four keys on her keyring: her house, her car, a post office box, all of which were square, and her office, thankfully, the only round one. She quickly unlocked the door and ran to her desk, slamming her thigh into the corner of it, giving herself a nasty charley horse.

No need to kill me, Roger, she thought, reeling from the pain; *I'm doing a bang-up job of that myself.*

Unable to see anything, Sylvie swung her hand out over the desk's surface, searching for the phone. She should have realized something was amiss when she didn't see the phone's ever-illuminated "call" button. It wasn't something on the forefront of her mind. She was in a panic, unable to think logically. Her only thoughts were of getting help.

Rummaging across her desk, she found the receiver and pulled it to her ear but heard only silence where a dial tone should have been. The display screen, which always lit up when the handset was off the base, remained dark.

"No, no, no," she muttered, frantically pressing the switch hook a few times, hoping for a dial tone. One never came. With dread, she felt for the phone's cord. Once locating it, her fingers hurriedly followed it off the side of her desk, then along the floor and across the wall's baseboard, until she discovered the reason for the phone's deadening silence. A shiver ran down her spine as the cut cord dangled from her fingers.

He was already here, she thought, *making sure I couldn't call out. But how? The door was locked.*

A flurry of thoughts swept across her mind until she landed on the only thing that made sense.

Venessa.

The facility's security guards had master keys for all the locks. Venessa's slumped body flashed into her head as she imagined Roger squatting over the woman's bloody corpse, smiling fiendishly, delighted in his handiwork, freeing the large keyring from her belt loop.

"Fuck," she whispered.

Sylvie started breathing heavier, grasping for her chest.

Keep calm, keep calm. Fuck!

Then it came to her.

The other office, she thought. *The other office has a phone. Maybe Roger didn't think to look there.*

Sylvie rushed to the door and quietly stepped back out into the hallway. She pressed her back to the wall and shimmied to her right toward the other office, trying not to make any noise. She could hear Roger's disturbing grunts and wheezes coming from the direction of the stairs as the sound echoed off the cinder block walls straight into her soul. He was there with her – in the basement. She couldn't see him, but he was there. All she could do was listen to his labored breathing as she held fast against the wall, slowly sliding her way to the next door, keeping her eyes peeled into the darkness behind her. She knew it was senseless since it was like peering into a black hole, but it kept her calm enough to continue toward the vacant office. She even started believing she'd make it.

That was *before* the lights kicked on, inopportunely giving away her location.

Roger had been standing a few feet from the bottom of the staircase, staring forward, when the lights suddenly burst to life. His hunched posture gave the appearance he had been squinting into the darkness, focused down the bathroom's corridor, hoping to see any movement. Sylvie's eyes grew wide while she watched in slow motion as his head slowly turned in her direction.

"Oh, there you are," he said menacingly, his eyes shooting needles at her.

"Stay away from me," Sylvie yelled, letting her eyes stray from her aggressor to focus on her destination, the door's knob only four feet from her right hand. She dashed to the empty office; the door was slightly ajar, allowing her easy access. She quickly ducked inside, closed the door, locked it, and let out a gasp, the sound of Roger's footsteps on the concrete floor outside clamoring in her ears as he approached. Feeling a moment of relief inside the safety of the locked room, she closed her eyes and slumped backward, pressing her back heavily against the door. The moment was fleeting, however, as the realization struck that locks meant little to someone who possessed the keys.

In a panic, her heart racing, Sylvie eyed the bookcase to her left. It was bare but perhaps still heavy enough to use as a barrier. She pushed away from the door and squeezed herself into the gap between the bookcase and the side wall, planting her buttock firmly against the sheetrock for leverage. Giving the pressed wood structure a shove, it scraped across the floor until its side hit the doorknob, stopping its movement only a few inches into the door's frame.

"Shit," Sylvie let out.

She got in front of the bookcase and gave it just enough of a yank to pull it away from the knob to finish her task. As she went back to the side of the large case to continue pushing it forward, three raps on the door stabbed daggers into her stomach.

"You shouldn't have run from me, Sylvie," the grunting voice spoke.

"I'm calling the police, Roger," Sylvie yelled, thrusting the bookcase in front of the door. "You should get back to your room."

She rested her head against the bookcase, listening to Roger's heavy breathing through the closed door, hoping to hear it slowly fade away as he obeyed her command.

It wasn't to be.

"They can't save you," the harsh voice said as the knob jangled in his grip. "I think you know that already. You're beyond saving. Just open the door."

With those foreboding words, Sylvie lifted her head from its rested position and glanced toward the desk. Her heart thumped, and she felt a pounding in the back of her skull. The phone, which had been in the empty office since she vacated it, was gone. The heavy breathing, again, took her ears hostage. Only this time, she realized the heavy breathing she heard was her own.

Fuck, fuck, fuck, she thought, her eyes shifting around the small space, her mind irrationally thinking maybe the phone had somehow mysteriously fallen to the floor. Her thoughts were snapped back to reality when Roger pounded his fist against the door, causing Sylvie to jump.

"Open the fucking door, Sylvie," Roger seethed. "I told you before; you can't stop what's coming."

Roger's threatening words were enough to startle Sylvie into action. Without a phone to call for help, she was trapped. She was going to have to wait it out. She knew the bookcase wouldn't be enough to keep Roger out for long. She needed something heavier to barricade herself in until somebody could rescue her. The desk was too large and cumbersome. Her lack of physical strength and the screaming pain in her lower back made moving it an obvious obstacle. Her eyes immediately jumped to the filing cabinets along the back wall. Individually, they were light enough for her to move. When put together, she hoped their combined weight might be enough to prevent Roger from busting in.

She ran to the cabinet on the left – the one most available for her to get a solid grip on – and slid her fingers into the tiny space behind it. Pulling it forward only a few inches, it made an awful screeching noise on the floor, like nails on a chalkboard, sending a shiver across her shoulders and down her arms. Her thoughts immediately thrust backward, the painful sound reminiscent of the scraping noise she'd heard and investigated earlier that morning.

Fighting through the unpleasantness she felt from the scuffing sound of metal on concrete, Sylvie yanked on the cabinet a second time, pulling it away from the wall several feet.

Sylvie's eyes widened in shock.

"What the hell?" she stated, staring down at a gaping hole cut into the sheetrock wall behind where the cabinet stood. The rough opening started just above the floor and was almost as wide as the cabinet. Its height was about equal to its width and large enough for a medium-sized dog to pass through. More disturbing, and what pulled Sylvie's attention away from the large gape itself, was the rope that had been snaked through the opening and attached to the cabinet's backside, weaved through two holes in the sheet metal and tied into a knot.

Sylvie instantly knew what it meant. The sound she'd heard before – she *wasn't* alone in the basement, after all. Someone had been in that office and escaped through the hole, using the rope to pull the cabinet back into place to conceal their exit.

With her thoughts no longer focused on Roger, she squatted beside the hole and peered through the opening with cautious eyes. It appeared to lead into the section of the basement that had been closed off years earlier.

Just then, Roger banged on the door again, yelling.

"Come out of there! You're only causing yourself more trouble."

Sylvie looked at the blocked doorway, then back into the hole. Roger would eventually find a way in. She wasn't so naïve to think she would remain safe, barricaded in that office. The hole, at least, offered her an escape, though to what or where she had no idea.

Roger's pounding continued, matching the pounding she felt in her chest. She quickly weighed her options: stay and die at the hands of a psychotic patient with tendencies toward violence and sexual sadism, or crawl through a hole in the wall into an unknown place to find who knows what. She didn't care for either, but with Roger's incessant pounding becoming more violent with each passing second, the choice became clear.

She stuck her head through the opening to get a sense of her surroundings, then crawled the rest of the way through.

Chapter 25

The Bowels

It was another world that Sylvie had just crawled into, one draped in gray concrete and stale air - a part of the hospital that had been closed off for over a dozen years. The musty smell permeated her nostrils, causing her nose to itch as she brushed away the sheetrock dust from her palms. The floor beyond the large hole in the wall was covered in it, as were the knees of her pants. Just inside the opening, jagged pieces of sheetrock were stacked into two piles, teetering like makeshift Jenga towers ready to topple. A thick rope, bathed in the white dust, lay at her feet on the cold floor, one end balled into a knot, the other trespassing through the sizeable gape and fixed to the rear of the filing cabinet.

216

Light bled into the pale space from the opening, giving Sylvie partial sight of the hospital's hidden lair, a scuffed trail of white powder deposited from a fleeing squatter disappearing beyond the light's reach. She scanned the colorless dungeon, where she imagined all sorts of unspeakable things once took place within its confines. She recalled the stories she'd heard of the old surgical room, where unrestrained electroshock treatment and impromptu lobotomies were performed on unwilling participants, those patients whose behavior was considered abhorrent and their "sickness" deemed incurable. She shivered at the thought.

She looked past the light into the gray void and closed her eyes, listening for any sound of an unwelcome tenant, or perhaps, the faint echoes of past screams embedded in the walls, the terrified wails of those begging to be free of their restraints. To Sylvie's relief, it was silent.

But the silence didn't last.

"Open the damn door!" Roger's voice boomed from the other side of the hole, accompanied by the pounding of his raging fist against the wooden surface. Sylvie jerked nervously, having briefly forgotten her dire situation.

"Just remember, Doctor; I warned you," the voice added. "There will be consequences." The pounding on the door began anew.

With anxiety quickly creeping back into her, Sylvie crouched by the hole and peered through to welcome the sight of the bookshelf still in place. But, like the silence, she knew it wouldn't last. She reached for the chalky rope and tugged at it, pulling the filing cabinet back into place and trapping her within the gloomy, gray prison.

Without the invading light from the connecting office, Sylvie found herself in complete darkness, save for a slight glimmer bending from around a far corner. The glow reflected from silver ductwork on the ceiling, giving her the hint of a path to follow. She stretched her arm out to her right, feeling for the wall. Her hand landed on a large steel pipe hung horizontally along the concrete that spanned the entirety of the wall. Flakes of rusted metal chipped under her touch and fell to the floor. With the rope still in her hand, she feverishly tied it around the steel pipe to keep the cabinet from being pulled away from the wall.

Hopefully, that will hold him off a bit, Sylvie thought.

Gathering her wits, she looked toward the faint glow ahead of her and took her first steps into the unknown darkness. As she slowly trodded forward, carefully sliding her fingers across the aged pipe, she realized how wrong she'd been during her time at Somerset. She'd always considered her office as being located in the bowels of the hospital. Regrettably, she now knew the truth; *this* was the hospital's bowels.

Sylvie trudged forward, following a single sliver of light as her only guide, promising hope of a lighted exit. She recognized that the light she saw poking its way into sight from around the corner was simply the end of its reach. Her interest, however, was in its origin.

As she neared the corner, where the path she'd been following took a sharp right, a subtle outline of a large door came into view from the light's dull radiance splashing across the far wall. Made of thick steel and looking like something out of an *actual* dungeon, its oxidized surface loomed before her, giving her pause. A small, square open window in the upper center, with steel bars crisscrossing in front of it like a tic tac toe game, caught her attention. Though the light didn't pierce into the darkness beyond the intimidating window (nor would she have wanted it to), she knew what the room was - the awful secrets it held. She could almost hear the anguished cries of the tortured souls who entered as troubled human beings and exited as something slightly less than — but still troubled. She couldn't let the eerie sight or the terrifying thoughts dissuade her from pushing on.

At the corner, she pressed her right shoulder into the wall, slowing her breathing before committing to taking a peek around it. She closed her eyes and began whispering to herself a familiar phrase she hadn't spoken in years. "Not the bad man, not the bad man, not the bad man."

She opened her eyes and let out a heavy breath. Then, she reached forward with her left hand and wrapped her fingers around the concrete corner, slowly leaning her head forward until a single eye could capture the setting.

Her instantaneous expression of dread would have been enough, even without the verbal confirmation.

"Oh, fuck!"

Leaving caution behind her, Sylvie sprang forward into the new hallway, where the ray of light in the distance rained down from another opening higher up in the wall above a steel ladder fastened to the concrete. Her reaction wasn't from the opening or the incoming light but rather from what the light revealed to her at the foot of the ladder.

Dressed in olive green garb, a psychiatric attendant was lying on the floor, facing away from her, tucked into a fetal position. As Sylvie ran toward him, she could see crimson smudges soaked into the visible side of his garment. Her thoughts immediately jumped to Tremont until she caught a glimpse of the man's Caucasian skin color.

"I'm here. Shit, I'm here."

She squatted behind the body and rolled him toward her to better assess the situation. When she saw, she fell backward onto her buttocks from the shock. There was nothing she could do except mutter the attendant's name.

"Samuel."

The man's face was as white as a sheet, his lips and chin covered in blood that had spilled from his mouth. Blotches of blood seeping through a half dozen tear marks on the chest of his shirt gave Sylvie a horrifying picture of what had happened. Samuel had been stabbed to death, the wounds still trickling blood and staining the concrete beneath him. Sylvie began to breathe heavier as she felt her arms turn to lead and drop to the floor, which caused immediate pain to shoot from the back of her hand, reminding her of her own injury.

Ignoring the pain, Sylvie glanced upward from the dead attendant, her focus shifting to a means of escape. The hole in the wall overhead, where the light shone through to expose Samuel's body to her, led to somewhere on the main floor. It was her only chance.

Somehow mustering the strength to peel her heavy limbs from the concrete floor, Sylvie stood and gazed at the steel ladder fixed to the wall, its rungs scraped clean of rust from recent use. Pieces of sheetrock lay below the bottom rung, unstacked and in disarray, dropped from the cut wall above. Beside the crumbled chunks of white, shattered shards of black plastic and electronic components were scattered in front of her, resolving the mystery of the missing phone. She grabbed hold of one of the ladder's steel legs and yanked on it as if unsure of its strength to hold her. Even in its severely corroded condition, it didn't budge. She shook her head in disbelief that something like this could even be happening to her.

It wasn't supposed to be like this, she thought.

She looked up at the hole, the light from the other side calling to her, taunting her. She looked back at Samuel's bloody corpse, the second one she'd seen that night. What was she to do? It was all a nightmare. She then looked back up, determining the hole was her only option of getting out of there alive. Then, with slight trepidation, Sylvie placed her foot on the bottom rung.

Chapter 26

No Escape

Pulling herself up to the top of the ladder, Sylvie peered through the break in the wall, but her view was partially obstructed. Like the hole in the lower office, something large had been placed in front of the opening to keep it hidden from sight, but the large object had been shifted away from the wall just enough to allow light to enter, or more accurately, for a person to squeeze through.

From her new vantage point, Sylvie could see that the light cascading into the abandoned lower chamber wasn't coming from the room she was looking into but from an area just beyond it. She removed one hand from the ladder, placed it against the smooth surface of the object in her way, and gave it a shove. It didn't move, but the force almost succeeded in knocking her backward off the ladder. Had her other hand not been clinging to the cold, steel rung for dear life, she would have joined the dead attendant below. A scene instantly flashed through her thoughts, one of her falling to the floor below, only to have Samuel's bloody body cushion her fall, saving her from her own gruesome death. She glanced down at the man's body, his lifeless eyes staring up at her as if pleading for her not to leave him. She quickly squeezed her eyes shut and leaned her forehead against the ladder, its cold surface calming her. She hadn't known Samuel that well, but she'd had a few conversations with him on occasion whenever their shifts overlapped. He seemed like a nice man. Then, she recalled a conversation they'd had once. He'd mentioned how he had joint custody of his sixteen-year-old daughter, Paige, who stayed with him every other week, and she wondered if this was one of those weeks. She imagined the young teen in her bedroom, texting her friends, unaware that anything had even happened to her father, then waking the next morning to an empty apartment, or worse, to police officers knocking on the door, there to deliver the awful news. It was a terrible thought, one she was all too familiar with.

Sylvie snapped her eyes open and glared at the obstacle in her way. She gave it a second shove but to no avail. She knew it had to be movable; after all, someone else had done it, but from her position and with only one hand, she had neither the strength nor the leverage. She concluded she'd have to squeeze through the tiny space between the heavy object and the wall.

She took another step up the ladder to where she could reach her arms farther through the hole. With one hand grabbing the corner of the impeding object, and her other arm wedged against the inside of the wall, Sylvie pulled her abdomen up to the higher floor and shimmied her weight forward until her legs dangled free of the ladder. With another tug, she pulled herself through enough to get her knees under her.

With the worst behind her, she forcefully pushed her way into the room from behind the heavy object, barely managing to squeeze her hips through the small gap.

You just had to have those last few spoonfuls of ice cream last night, she thought, bringing levity to the situation she'd found herself in. It was her safety mechanism to keep from going mad from sheer terror.

She stood from her knees, her lower back screaming at her, reminding her how painful wooden stair treads could be from improper use. She hadn't the time to dwell on it.

She quickly scanned the room and realized she was in the old, defunct kitchen. The heavy item she fought with was the oversized, stainless steel refrigerator that, even empty, felt like she was trying to move an elephant. The room was dim, receiving light from the brightened hallway beyond the plastic sheeting draped in front of the open doorway.

She was grateful it had been enough to get her out of the concrete bowels.

The kitchen was cold and unwelcoming, with its plain white tile floor and stainless steel counters and appliances crammed into such a small space. In the center of the room, taking up the majority of the area - and, in the process, blocking a straight path to the exit - was a behemoth of a prep table, also made of stainless steel. It stood on four thick, tubular legs and had a lower shelf stacked high with burn-stained pots and pans. She shivered at the coldness. She knew it was the fear that had crept into her, causing chills to race down her spine, but the room would get the blame.

Then, as the anxiety of being trapped in the lower levels subsided, it came to her in a flash.

The lights, she thought, her eyes open wide. *The power is on. The scanners will work.*

With a thought of desperation, she darted around the side of the prep table, heading for the exit. As she rounded its front corner, her foot caught on something, causing her to fall forward and smash her knee into the hard tile.

"Ah, fuck!" she screamed, grabbing her knee and squeezing her face tight in pain, clenching her jaw so tensely her cheeks hurt. She turned onto her side to look at what she'd tripped on, her face still wincing from the throbbing in her knee. At the sight, she felt her blood run cold and her stomach churn, fighting to hold down its contents.

At her feet, the staff night nurse lay sprawled on the floor, her uniform bathed in blood. The nurse, whose outstretched arm Sylvie tripped on, was facing up, her neck sliced from ear to ear. She had stab wounds all along her upper chest and side. A trail of blood leading in from the hallway suggested she'd been dragged there after having been killed. Sylvie covered her mouth as she felt liquid rise into her esophagus. It was all she could do to keep herself from throwing up.

Closing her eyes, Sylvie felt a tear escape and roll down her cheek. She swallowed heavily to push the rising contents of her stomach back down where it belonged. She then opened her eyes and steered them away from the nurse's dead body, hoping to avoid a sudden discharge of the early evening's dinner.

Rolling back onto her palms, doing everything she could to keep her aching knee from touching the floor, Sylvie pushed herself upright onto one leg. She lowered the other, softly pressing the soul of her foot against the floor to see if she could put weight on it. It was sore, and she'd be hobbling for a while, but the pain was manageable.

As she was about to take a step toward the plastic barrier, another sudden pain shot through her body, one so extreme that her voice failed her as she opened her mouth to scream. Her body immediately crumpled back to the floor, once again, her knee hitting the tile. She didn't feel it as much that second time as the pain in her other leg fully gripped her senses.

She looked down at her lower leg and saw blood streaming from her ankle, filling the back of her shoe. Her Achilles tendon had just been sliced through. As Sylvie sat in utter pain, staring at the red liquid seeping from her new wound, a slight movement from beyond her outstretched leg caught her attention.

From under the prep table's lower shelf, a pallid-looking, wrinkly arm emerged wielding a butcher's knife, its blade tainted with red.

"What the fuck? What the fuck?" she murmured, her eyes bulging from her sockets in horror. Unable to watch whatever it was crawling out into the open, Sylvie turned herself onto her knees, ignoring the excruciating pain shooting from her kneecap and ankle. Her only thought was of escaping.

Crawling on her hands and knees, her foot limp and dragging, leaving a trickling trail of blood on the floor, Sylvie franticly thrust herself through the hanging sheet of plastic into the lighted hallway. Her thoughts scrambled for a way out. It was a quick left to the end of the hall, then a sharp right to a straightaway, leading to the Day Room. If she could make it there, she'd have more room to move, more places to hide. In the hallway, she knew she was a sitting duck. Unable to walk and in agonizing pain, it would be a hard-fought battle to get there, but with the ungodly sound of the knife scraping across the floor behind her, it was a battle she was ready to fight.

Chapter 27

Nobody Can Know

The whispers were calling to her, but she refused to look back while laboring to crawl her way to safety.

"Sylvie."

The door into the activities hall was just up ahead. She was almost there. She could hear and feel her breathing increase with each painful movement.

"Oh, Sylvie."

From behind her, accompanying the hoarse whispers, she could hear the footsteps of her stalker slowly sliding across the floor, taking their time as if playing a game of cat and mouse. She, of course, was the mouse, trying to escape into her little hole before the cat could catch her and eat her alive.

"Come now, Doctor."

With each crawling shuffle she took, the pain alternated between her throbbing knee and the burning sensation she felt shooting from her ankle.

"You're only delaying the inevitable."

Sylvie paused at the intersecting hallway on her right, down which the doctors' offices were located. She took a glance, hoping to see someone who might be able to help her. It was empty. She pressed forward to the locked door of the Day Room, pressing her blood-stained palm to the glass to keep herself from falling forward while she retrieved her badge from her pants pocket. She stretched her arm upward and flashed it in front of the scanner, listening for the clicking sound as the light turned green. Pushing the door open, she fell back to her palms and began crawling through it into the large room. Unfortunately, she was only halfway through the open door when she suddenly felt a hand grip the bottom of her bloody ankle's pant leg and tug on it, preventing her from continuing. She let out a scream and flailed her other leg, suppressing the numbing pain in her knee, wildly kicking backward, hoping to hit her assailant. It wasn't until she aggressively yanked on her held leg that she broke free from her attacker's tight grasp. She felt its release immediately when her foot fell to the floor, sending a stinging shockwave through her entire body from her injured ankle. As much as the surging pain in her limbs urged her not to move, she lunged herself through the doorway. Without so much as a glance back, she quickly kicked the door shut behind her and slid herself to the right, out of view from the hallway. She rolled onto her backside to sit up and watched the scanner light turn red as it locked.

She slid herself backward on her hands, using her one semi-good leg to push with, while she stared at the scanner's glowing light. She tried to calm her heartbeat, which felt like a jackhammer in her chest. A bleak thought crossed her mind - knowing her luck, she'd probably have a heart attack before the killer could get to her. Whoever it was couldn't see her, just as she couldn't see them. She had no idea if they were even still in the hallway. As if in answer to her unspoken contemplation, she watched in terror as the red light on the scanner flickered to green.

"No, no, no, no, no," she mumbled, shaking her head hysterically while continuing to push herself backward toward the front window and the other exit. Sylvie watched a hand shove the door open, and without a thought of the unbearable pain she felt, she immediately flipped around onto her palms and scuttled past the nurses' station as quickly as she could toward the other door.

Sylvie had almost reached her destination when the hum of the generator ceased. The hospital became blanketed in darkness. Overhead, the emergency exit lights kicked on, showering the room in a reddish hue. Not accepting her circumstances, Sylvie waved her badge at the second door's scanner several times, silently pleading for it to unlock. Tears streamed down her face as she slammed her fist against the reinforced glass door.

"Somebody, help me!" she screamed, gazing out into the deserted hallway, her body trembling with fear. "Help me, please," she begged to nobody, letting her hand slide down the glass, creating a squealing sound. Then, she became silent.

The heavy breathing gave it away; she wasn't alone.

"Gotcha," the whisper said, followed by forced laughter.

Sylvie jolted to her left, falling back against the room's front plate glass window, her eyes sharply focused on the source of the laughter.

Standing before her, the threat she believed to be a single person had become two as the shadowy figures stood above her, their darkened silhouettes outlined with a red aura from the exit signs behind them.

"I told you she wasn't special," the familiar voice said.

"Never you mind," replied the other.

Just then, the lights kicked back on, causing Sylvie to squint as her eyes adjusted to the light. It didn't matter; she already recognized the voices.

Greta Lambeau and Mrs Landry stared down at Sylvie's cowering form, cackling like old hens.

"Look at her," Greta said, pointing the knife in Sylvie's direction. "She's just like the rest – weak and pitiful."

"I thought you were different," Mrs. Landry belted out.

Sylvie looked up, terrified of the two women.

"Why are you doing this?"

"Can you believe this fucking girl?" Greta questioned, waving the knife in a circular motion. "*Why are you doing this?*" the older woman repeated snarkily, mocking the doctor.

"I'll tell you why," Mrs. Landry jumped in, leaning heavily on her cane. "Because you're out there," she pointed to the large window, "while we're locked away in here."

"We were supposed to be out of this shithole," Greta interjected. "But as usual, they lied to us. Everybody lies to us. Just like my Henry did."

"Your Henry?" Sylvie stated, hoping to talk the women down. "Henry Gaston. Your agent."

"My agent, my lover. He got what was coming to him."

Sylvie nodded. "He *did* get what was coming to him. He beat you. You acted in self-defense."

"He beat me?" Greta questioned, a look of confusion on her face. Then she understood. "Oh, that's right. I'd forgotten about that. You *did* read my file, after all. And here I thought you were all talk." Greta began laughing, to which Mrs. Landry followed suit.

"She's a funny one, isn't she," Mrs. Landry added through her laughter, applying for Greta's recognition. Sylvie didn't know to whom the comment was directed. Looking at Mrs. Landry's confused expression, she was unsure if even the older woman knew herself.

Greta started again. "That man never beat me. He just held me back. I was going to be big. But he couldn't get over his jealousy of my success. I did what I had to do. He came into my trailer that day, thinking he could drop me like I was some piece of trash. He threatened to leave me. Well, nobody leaves Greta Lambeau. She's the goddamn star of the show." Greta threw her arms up into the air, smiling like she was performing in front of a crowd. Then, just as quickly, the smile faded as she peered into Sylvie's eyes with disdain. "I sliced the fucker!"

"Isn't she fabulous?" Mrs. Landry added, applauding. "A wonderful performance."

"You're sick," Sylvie whispered.

"What was that?" Greta asked, placing the knife behind her ear and pushing a flap of it forward with the blade. "I didn't quite catch that."

"You're crazy. You're both crazy. You belong in here."

"Oh, honey," Greta said, devilishly smirking at the terrified doctor. "You haven't *seen* crazy yet. Just wait. We're only getting started."

Chapter 28

You Should Have Known

*H*ow did everything get so fucked up, Sylvie thought.

How was she in her current predicament? She should have never gone to the hospital during the off-shift.

Why, her thoughts continued to question. *Why did I need to find proof of anything? It's not like anyone would have listened to me.*

Whatever was going on with Dr. Prichard and the patients, it wasn't her problem. She'd had a plan; she should have stuck to it. It was the only thing that should have mattered. But she was also a doctor. She couldn't sit idly by when she knew something wasn't right. She felt compelled to *make* it her problem. And now, in the worst possible way, it was.

"Greta, you don't want to do this," Sylvie said, hoping to reason with the knife-wielding woman. "I'm here to help you."

"That's the problem with all you doctors," Greta responded. "You all think I need help. I don't need any of you. I like the way I am. But look at you, with your pretty, young face, frightened and teary-eyed, unable to even walk to save yourself. No, I'm not the one who needs help now, am I?"

"That's right," Mrs. Landry chimed in. "Greta doesn't need your help. She's great. It's right there in her name."

Sylvie shook her head in disgust, holding back tears that would boil and evaporate should they stream down her cheeks with how heated she was at the moment.

"Are you kidding me right now?" Sylvie raised her voice in defiance. "You don't think you need help? You killed the nurse. You killed Samuel. You killed Venessa. Don't you understand that? They're all dead. *You* did that," she said, pointing at Greta. She hoped it would snap the crazed woman back to reality.

The older woman stood up straight and held her chin up proudly. "They got what was coming to them. They were holding me back. All of them. You too. Just like Henry did. He got his. You'll get yours too. You all have kept me locked away like a caged animal, and an animal is never more dangerous than when trapped in a corner. But now I know better. Dr. Prichard promised me I'd be a star again. He's the only one who cares, the only one who gets me. He understands my true talent."

"Dr. Prichard?" Sylvie mumbled. Then, like a battering ram, it hit her. She recalled her earlier conversation with Nurse Sullivan about how Dr. Prichard prescribed a supplemental drug, Ditrolazipan Sulfate, to some patients. It was the same drug given to Roger at Teton and the same given to Mr. Hoklin before his outburst. When she questioned who had already received the drug, she remembered Nurse Sullivan mentioning Greta, only, at the time, she was too fixated on Mr. Hoklin's abnormal behavior to think much of it.

"This isn't you, Greta," Sylvie stated, staring up at the two women. "It's the medication you took. It's making you act this way."

"You shut your mouth," Mrs. Landry yelled, waving her finger back and forth. Sylvie recoiled at the gesture. "Greta doesn't need medication to act. She's an incredible actress. She played the magnificent Maggie Deetweiler. That woman was something else, helping children find homes. You know, my sister and I grew up in an orphanage. We could have used a woman like her."

"Did you take the special medication, too, Mrs. Landry?" Sylvie spoke mildly, appealing to the woman's softer side.

"What if I did?" was her answer. "Dr. Prichard said it can make me whole again."

"Make you whole again?" Sylvie questioned. "Dr. Prichard lied to you," she added, trying to shift the focus and anger away from her. "He lied to both of you. He doesn't care about either of you; he's only looking out for himself. You must see that. He's not trying to help you. He has some special interest in the medication he prescribed to you. Think about it, Mrs. Landry. What does that even mean, 'make you whole again'?"

"It means I ain't been whole since they took my sister from me," the woman snarled.

"Took your sister from you?" Sylvie repeated, confused at the woman's response. "You killed her, Mrs. Landry. That's why you're here. You killed your sister shortly after you left the boarding school."

"What did you just say to me?" Mrs. Landry screeched, bending over and slapping the doctor across the face. Sylvie pressed her hand against her cheek to dull the pain just as tears leaked from her eyes. "You're just like those sons of bitches who wouldn't listen to me back then. I didn't kill my sister; she took her own life. I don't even belong in here."

Still holding her palm firmly to her face, Sylvie softly questioned the deranged woman while Greta looked on from over Mrs. Landry's shoulder.

"Why? Why would your sister do that?"

"Because she was stupid," the woman snapped. "And because she wanted me to be happy. She wanted me to live my life, to get married to Thomas, and live happily ever after. All she did was nag, nag, nag me about it, but she knew I could never leave her."

"So, you couldn't leave her," Sylvie said sympathetically. "You cared for her; I get it. We've all cared for someone like that. But why would she kill herself? If your sister truly felt that strongly about it, she could have just walked away. *She* could have left *you*. She didn't need to kill herself."

Mrs. Landry looked up at the ceiling and threw her hands in the air, frustrated. "You just don't get it, do you, you stupid bitch."

Greta began laughing and pointing the knife at Sylvie. "For a doctor," she said, "you're not too bright. Looks like all that listening you do has gotten you nowhere." Then she looked at her friend and nodded. "Go ahead, Trudy; show her."

Mrs. Landry whipped her head toward Greta, "I told you not to call me that. My sister called me Trudy. It's Gertie."

"Whatever." Greta rolled her eyes, brushing off the woman's comment. "Just show her."

Mrs. Landry turned her attention to Sylvie and stepped back a few steps to stand beneath an overhead light. She reached down, grabbed the bottom hem of her pull-over scrub shirt, and unabashedly peeled it up and over her head to reveal her naked torso. Without Sylvie realizing it, her jaw dropped several inches at the sight.

The septuagenarian's wrinkled upper body was a pale yellow, her thin frame displaying a road map of bluish veins splintering in all directions under her diaphanous skin. Her droopy left breast hung almost to her belly button. Her right breast was non-existent, replaced by a massive patch of hardened scar tissue, healed over by age. The scar, having a darker orange color, stood out compared to the rest of the woman's pale skin. It encompassed more than only her breast, originating above her right shoulder and streaking down like a jagged bolt of lightning to her hip, where it wrapped around her side and up her back in a loop. The scarred area wasn't indicative of merely a mastectomy to remove a cancerous breast. No, Mrs. Landry had something much larger removed.

"Do you get it now, you stupid sheep?" Mrs. Landry screeched, turning sideways to display the full extent of restorative surgery she'd undergone. "We *couldn't* leave each other. So instead, Cassie killed herself, nearly taking me with her."

"You . . . you were conjoined twins," Sylvie murmured, shocked by the discovery as much as the sight.

"Thoracopagus, they called it," Mrs. Landry explained. "We shared a liver, kidney, and part of the stomach and intestines. We were fine, though; we made it work. Until my sister couldn't any longer. I should have known, but I didn't. Or maybe I did but chose to ignore it.

"After we left the boarding school, we squatted in an abandoned apartment until we could figure out where to go. We'd been survivors all our lives. I knew we'd be okay as long as we had each other.

Cassie didn't feel that way, though. She was so afraid, so distraught. I thought I'd be able to get her through it, but she was so focused on me and Tommy that I missed it. She only wanted me to be happy, but she thought neither of us ever would be if we stayed together. She got ahold of a knife – I still don't know where from – and while I slept, she jabbed it into her neck. I awoke when the blood splashed across my face. I think she tried screaming, but only gurgling noises came out. I did enough screaming for both of us as I held her in my arms, trying to stop the bleeding.

"I never knew how heavy dead weight could be until I tried dragging myself out of that room, Cassie's limp form holding me down. I made it as far as the doorway into the hallway before my limbs gave out from the loss of blood. I was so weak.

"For what seemed like an eternity, I sat against the doorjamb, screaming for help, hoping my lungs wouldn't give out. I felt myself weakening, knowing my end was coming. I looked at my dead sister's bloody body slumped away from mine, and I couldn't bear to sit there and let myself slowly wither away. Without Cassie, I had nothing to live for. She was gone, and all I could think about was joining her. I grabbed the bloody knife still in her hand, wondering how painful it would be. I closed my eyes, ready to jab it into my neck the same way she had done it. That was when a hand grabbed my wrist, preventing me from ending my life. I didn't even hear the man approach. The next thing

I remember, I was in the hospital, and they were prepping me for surgery to remove my sister.

"My sister," Mrs. Landry lamented, dropping her chin to her bare chest. "Cassie always thought of others above herself. She thought if she were dead, I'd no longer have any excuses for why I was holding myself back. She didn't realize I would've died too, within hours, if I couldn't get medical help. The dummy; I almost did, anyway. I should have. I wanted to.

"They took her from me that day," the woman continued, scowling as she slid her shirt back on over her shoulders. "They cut her from me like she was a cancerous tumor.

"She took herself," Greta stated unemotionally.

"Never you mind," Mrs. Landry yelled, pointing her finger angrily at Greta.

"Don't you take that tone with me," Greta returned. "Remember who you're talking to. I'm the one who hatched this plan."

Mrs. Landry offered a snide retort, which was returned in kind by Greta. As the women began arguing, Sylvie stopped listening to their bickering, her eyes shifting to the door on her left, the electronic scanner almost within her reach. With the two women distracted, she was sure she could unlock the door and make it out before they could stop her. Even with her injuries, she had to try. Her thoughts ran wild.

I've still got one mostly good leg, she thought, trying to remain positive in an impossible situation. *I only need to get out that door.*

Then, doubt and negativity crept in.

Yeah, right. Then another door and another door. I'll never make it. They'll catch me.

Then, reason slowly swept in.

No, I'm dead if I sit here. They've already killed. They'll do it again. I have to get out. I can do it. I'm not going to die like this. Be strong, Sylvie. Be the woman you came here to be.

She glanced at the distracted women, then back to the door again. Deciding it was her only chance, Sylvie lunged for the door, her badge in hand to unlock it.

Chapter 29

I'll Never Tell

She got as far as watching the light turn green before the blade of the knife slashed across her hand, immediately spilling blood. Sylvie reeled from the pain, falling back against the window while grabbing her hand and letting out a sharp cry as tears poured from her eyes.

"Why?" she screamed, coddling her hand against her chest, blood streaming over the fingers of the hand squeezing the wound. "Why are you doing this? I haven't done anything to you." Tears rolled down Sylvie's cheek and dripped from her chin, splashing against her blood-soaked hands.

"Fucker!" Greta scolded, pointing the knife at Sylvie. "Thought you could get away, did you? You think because we're old, we can't stop you?"

"Just let me go," Sylvie pleaded through tear-filled eyes, her sobbing, cracking voice studdering and barely audible. "I won't tell anyone. I don't even need to come back. I can leave, and nobody will know anything. I shouldn't have even come here. It was all a mistake. I shouldn't be here. Please, just let me leave."

"What the fuck are you babbling about?" Greta questioned, moving the knife in a figure-eight formation in front of Sylvie's face while Mrs. Landry giggled behind her. "'*I shouldn't be here*,'" Greta mocked in a ridiculing voice. "Then why the fuck are you here?" she questioned. "You think *we're* the crazy ones? Who in their right mind would ever come to work in this hellhole?"

With tears still falling, Sylvie dropped her chin and looked down at her bloody hands. They were trembling, but not from pain or fear, and no matter how hard she tried, she couldn't get them to stop.

"It . . ," Sylvie began, stumbling with her words. "It was . . ,"

"Oh, for Christ's sake," the crazed woman snarled. "We ain't got all night. Spit it out already."

"It was for my parents, all right," Sylvie yelled, keeping her head down. "I'm here because of my parents."

"Well, la di fucking da," Greta teased. "I'm sure your parents are so proud of you. They probably tell all their high society friends how their daughter is a doctor, thinking they're better than everyone else. I picture their snooty asses sipping from their wine glasses, pleased as pigs in shit at how their wonderful daughter turned out. What did they do, force you to come here so you could see how the other half lived?"

Sylvie shook her head, clenching her teeth. "Shut up."

"Does that upset you, princess?" Greta chided. "Am I hurting your delicate feelings? Well, too fucking bad. You probably had everything handed to you. Mommy and Daddy's precious little girl."

"Shut up," Sylvie said again, closing her eyes tight, trying to ignore the woman's words.

"I bet you call them every night to tell them how the crazies are, making yourselves even more important than you already think you are."

"The crazies," Mrs. Landry repeated from over Greta's shoulder. "That's us."

"I imagine Mommy and Daddy are sitting by the phone now, waiting with bated breath for their little darling to call. Like they've got nothing better to do than to listen to all the gossip about the thrown out, locked away, forgotten people of the world."

Sylvie's tears stopped. Her breathing mellowed as she opened her eyes and lifted her chin from her chest, her cold eyes staring into Greta's.

"My parents are dead, you fucking bitch," Sylvie stated through clenched teeth.

Greta pulled back, surprised at Sylvie's response. If she had a remorseful look on her face, it quickly faded. She curled her upper lip and responded, "Boo hoo. Your parents are dead. So what. Everybody dies. Our parents are dead." She waved the knife back and forth between herself and Mrs. Landry. "My Henry is dead, the son of a bitch. Gertrude's goddamn stupid sister is dead."

Mrs. Landry gave Greta a side-eyed glare.

"Get used to it, honey," Greta continued, "because soon, you'll be dead, too. Isn't that right, Trudy?"

"I told you before; it's Gertie," Mrs. Landry shouted. "Enough of this shit; give me the knife. I want to cut her, too."

Mrs. Landry reached for the knife, but Greta pulled her hand away before the woman could grab it.

"Hey!" Greta snapped. "Watch it. We want this done right. Of the two of us, I'm the one who knows what I'm doing. You couldn't even kill yourself after your sister died."

"That isn't fair," Mrs. Landry cried out. "We're supposed to be a team. The Gertie and Greta show."

"What the fuck are you yapping about?" Greta questioned, turning to Mrs. Landry. "We both know I'm the star of this show. Always have been; always will be. If anything, it should be the Greta and Gertie show."

"Bullshit!" Mrs. Landry responded. "It's Gertie and Greta. I came up with the name. It stays."

"The hell it does. It's Greta and Gertie. That's final." She turned back toward Sylvie, the doctor's frame cowering against the window, though her face still displaying anger.

"Fine," Mrs. Landry mumbled from behind Greta. "We'll *share* being the star."

Greta's eyes shifted sideways as a crazed look fell upon her face.

"What did you just say?" she hissed through gritted teeth. "Share being the star?"

She turned again to her partner in crime, her face showing more than anger or displeasure. It had changed to unadulterated rage.

"You think you can share *my* spotlight? Who the hell do you think you are? You're a nobody, a freak, an accident at birth. Even your own mother couldn't stand the sight of you. But me – I've *always* been the star of the show. I'm Greta fucking Lambeau, and nobody shares *my* spotlight. Nobody!"

Sylvie heard the sound for the first time. Her eyes widened, and her jaw dropped in horror as she watched Greta plunge the large knife, up to the handle, into Mrs. Landry's stomach. Blood poured from the woman's insides, washing over Greta's hand and dripping to the floor in a steady stream. Greta stared blankly into Mrs. Landry's confused eyes, the life slowly exiting the older woman's body through the large gash in her stomach.

"This is *my* show," Greta remarked a final time before pulling the knife from Mrs. Landry's gut, "and don't you ever forget about that." The woman's body slumped to the ground, the "Hero of the Hospital" dead before ever hitting the floor.

"Nooo!" Sylvie cried out. "What have you done?"

Greta turned back to Sylvie, the knife stained with Mrs. Landry's blood. She flashed a devious smile. As the crazed woman stepped forward, evil intentions shooting from her eyes, the lights again suddenly dimmed, flickered, and then went out. Greta stopped for a moment under the glowing exit sign overhead. She shifted her eyes upward, the red from the light reflecting off her irises, making her look like the possessed woman she was. The deranged woman then turned her stare back to her quivering prey, her eyes still bathed in the red glow.

"How fitting," Greta acknowledged, a drop of saliva falling from her lips.

"Now, where were we?"

Chapter 30

Late Arrival

The room's reddish glow did nothing to calm Sylvie's racing mind. Perhaps if it were pitch black, she would have felt better; she wouldn't see it coming (though she knew her mind would make it worse). Instead, the red hue of the exit lights splashed over the crazed, methodically approaching woman, displaying a terrifying view of a foreboding, knife-wielding fiend standing over her.

"Don't do this, Greta," Sylvie begged, shaking her head. "I know this isn't you. It's the medication they gave to you. Let me help you. You can be a star again. You can go to Hollywood. Let me help you achieve that dream."

It was a last-ditch effort, appealing to the woman's desire to be what she once was – what she almost had. Sylvie failed in her efforts to break through to the woman in their sessions, but maybe with Greta's mind altered by the effects of the Ditrolazipan, she could finally succeed.

Or maybe she couldn't, but she had to try.

"Oh, that shit?" Greta announced. "That stuff back there with Gertrude?" She flung her thumb over her shoulder to acknowledge the dead woman. Sylvie's eyes shifted to Mrs. Landry's body sprawled on the floor behind Greta, blood pouring from her stomach, pooling at her side. "That was all part of the act," the woman continued. "I *am* an actress, after all. Well, I *was*," she stated emphatically. "You have no idea what it's like to be in the limelight – to have thousands of adoring fans writing you letters, letting you know how much you've inspired them. It wasn't only that: the parties, the fancy hotels, the glitz, the glamour – it was all so glorious and wonderful. I know I'm never going to get that life back. Look at me; I'm in a goddamn loony bin with a bunch of crazy fucktards. And you, miss fancy-pants, with your *'I'm listening,'* and your *'let me help you,'* did nothing to get me out of here - nothing to show the world I'm still relevant."

"I can," Sylvie spoke, desperation in her voice. "I mean, I can try. Let me try. You're feeling down – I get that. You had everything going for you, but then, Henry betrayed you."

"You're goddamn right he did," Greta agreed.

"Right. We've all had our share of loss. You lost out on your chance to make it big in Hollywood. But that's not what this is about. It's about always getting let down. Henry – he let you down. Your fans let you down. But I'm here with you now, Greta. I'm here to tell you I won't let you down. Since the day I walked through those doors, right or wrong, I've been on your side. Yes, I'm your doctor, but I'm also a big fan of your movies. You were magnificent in the way you commanded the screen. But aside from all that, I hope you can believe me when I tell you I'm also your friend."

"My . . . friend?" Greta's eyebrows dropped as if she'd heard the word truthfully, perhaps for the first time. "You're paid to say those things. You don't care about me."

"I *do* care, Greta," Sylvie replied, nodding. She brought her arm to her face and wiped away the remaining tears clinging to her cheeks. "I told you – I listen to my patients."

Greta paused, looking back at Mrs. Landry's bloody corpse. Her tense shoulders dropped as if a sudden realization swept over her. She looked down at the knife in her hand, her eyes widening as she began to tremble.

"Oh my goodness," the woman mumbled, suddenly looking frightened. "What have I done?" She started crying.

The woman's legs began to shake uncontrollably. She looked confused and dizzy - as if she were about to faint. She bent over, reaching for the floor to prevent herself from falling forward. Balancing herself with her free hand, Greta slowly lowered herself until she was on her knees, straddling Sylvie's outstretched legs.

Sylvie winced from her ankle being jostled but kept her eyes focused on the knife. She'd seen what the woman was capable of.

"It's okay, Greta," Sylvie said, struggling through the pain. "I'm here with you. Give me the knife; we can figure this out together."

"The knife?" Greta questioned.

"That's right. The knife." Still holding her injured hand, Sylvie pointed.

Greta again looked down at the knife in her hand as if forgetting she'd still had it.

"Oh my God. The blood," Greta whimpered, her words barely audible through choked sobs. "I did it. It was me. How? Why?"

The woman looked terrified, perhaps painfully aware for the first time of what she'd done.

"Just give me the knife, Greta. It was all a mistake. We can make it all go away if you give me the knife. I'm here for you. I want to help you."

Greta looked at Sylvie with soulful eyes as they began to fill with more tears. "You want to help me?"

Sylvie nodded. "Yes."

"I always knew you were a good person, dear." Greta smiled delicately. "And you know what else?"

Sylvie offered a slight grin. "What's that?"

The older woman gazed into Sylvie's eyes as her remorseful smile suddenly faded to a sickening scowl. Sylvie's heart dropped into her stomach.

"I know a liar when I see one," Greta screamed as she jabbed the knife into Sylvie's thigh.

Sylvie howled in pain, "Ow! Fuck, fuck! Nooo!"

Out of instinct, or perhaps shock, she shoved the woman back, causing Greta to yank the knife free of Sylvie's leg. The doctor screamed out in excruciating agony. No tears fell from Sylvie's eyes as she clutched her leg tightly and watched the crazy woman stand upright, a pleased smirk on her face.

"That's just a taste of the pain you'll feel," Greta stated, her lip curled. "Soon, you'll know all the pain I've felt over the years – the pain caused by people like you."

Just then, Sylvie noticed Greta's eyes shift to the window above her head. Before she could react, something pounded on the pane behind her, causing her upper body, which had been up against the glass, to jump forward.

"Sylvie!" a familiar voice cried out.

Even muffled through thick glass, never had she heard a sweeter voice of salvation. She turned her head to see young Kevin staring in at her, his palms pressed against the reinforced glass.

"Kevin," Sylvie shouted weakly, bringing her bloody palm to the glass to match his, smearing the red liquid downward as her hand slipped. "Run and get help, Kevin."

The boy's eyes widened at the sight of the streaking blood on the glass, frightened by what he'd just arrived to.

"Get help, Kevin," Sylvie shouted a second time, staring into the boy's terrified eyes.

Kevin nodded, then glanced over Sylvie's head. The look of terror in the boy suddenly intensified as he excitedly tapped his index finger against the window repeatedly, his wide-eyed stare focused beyond her.

"Sylvie, behind you!" he shouted.

Sylvie quickly turned her head, expecting the woman to be on top of her in a heartbeat. Instead, she saw a shadowy figure behind Greta, partially obscured by the older woman. Sylvie's first thought came out in words.

"Thank God, Tremont."

Greta almost had a chance to turn her head before the pointed end of a broken broomstick pierced through her chest from behind. She let out an ungodly gasp as her chest heaved and her chin shot skyward. Sylvie's body convulsed uncontrollably at the sight.

Just as quickly as the broom handle entered Greta's body, it was yanked from it, splattering blood in a line across the floor. The older woman's body fell forward, hitting the floor and knocking the knife from her hand.

"Sylvie!" Kevin cried again. "It's him."

Without looking at the young boy, Sylvie again shouted an order to him. "Go, Kevin. Go now. Get out of here. Get help."

With only a brief hesitation, Kevin quickly ran off, unwillingly leaving his friend alone and in danger.

Sylvie sat with her back against the window, her heart racing, looking up at an even greater threat than the deranged woman lying at her feet. In all her fear and excitement, she thought she'd forgotten about him, but in truth, she couldn't forget; he was always there in the back of her mind. The man she feared most. Roger Loomis.

"Sylvie," the man began, licking his lower lip, "it's good that we're finally alone with nobody around to disturb us." He glanced down at the blood-soaked broomstick in his hand, the one he'd snatched from the downstairs closet, and let out a grunt that went straight through Sylvie, causing her to shiver from the worst fear she'd ever experienced. She no longer felt the stab wound in her leg as she sat frozen to her bones, unsure if she was going to pass out. "You and me," Roger continued, "we're going to have a little chat."

Chapter 31

Are You Listening?

Snapping back to reality, Sylvie realized there was no escaping this time, even if she'd had the strength. She was losing a good amount of blood; the liquid was seeping from her stabbed leg and absorbing into the fibers of her pants. Her hand squeezed her upper thigh above the wound to try and minimize the flow, but it was useless. Her hands were weak and burning from the cuts they'd sustained. Tears rolled down Sylvie's cheek as she let her head fall back against the window behind her, her thoughts succumbing to the idea that she wasn't long for this world. She hoped it would be quick or that she would soon surrender to the dark sleep from the blood loss. Wincing in pain, she glared up at the threatening figure standing over her, his face showing disdain and his grip squeezed so tight around the bloody broomstick that his veins were protruding from the back of his hand.

"The boy went to get help," Sylvie said, hoping to scare Roger into backing down and leaving her to die in peace. "They're going to be coming."

"We both know they'll never get here in time," Roger responded.

Sylvie's shoulders dropped, realizing it was no use. Roger wasn't going away. She tightened her face and squinted to hold back the tears that wanted to explode from her ducts. She stared angrily into the dangerous man's eyes, shooting daggers into him.

"Do what you're gonna do, fucker," Sylvie hissed through clenched teeth, her voice weakening.

Roger tilted his head to one side and smirked. "Oh, I intend to," he said calmly, "don't you worry about that. But first," he glanced down at her injured leg, watching her struggle to apply pressure, then shifted his eyes down to the fallen woman at his feet, the back of Greta's shirt torn through where he had impaled her, "let's get you fixed up, shall we? We wouldn't want you dying prematurely. Not before all the fun starts."

Roger squatted beside Greta, placing his makeshift weapon on the floor next to the older woman's dead body. Reaching his fingers into the hole in the back of her blood-soaked shirt, he gave a yank, tearing a large enough rip in the fabric to fit his other hand. Then, with both hands, he forcefully pulled at the material, peeling away a strip of Greta's lower shirt. Sylvie watched in horror as Greta's body flopped like a dying fish while Roger aggressively tugged at her clothing, tearing away a large section.

"This should do it," the man said, standing and letting the strip of red-stained material hang down from his hand. He stepped forward toward Sylvie, leaving the broomstick behind, something she noticed immediately. Her body began to quiver as Roger inched closer to her, the fabric of Greta's shirt dangling from his fingers.

"Get away from me," Sylvie yelled, trying to kick her good leg at him. It barely moved as excruciating pain shot through her body from the slightest attempt. Her body stiffened, and her head reeled, slamming against the thick glass.

"You'd better calm down before you do even more harm to yourself," Roger stated, kneeling over Sylvie's ankle, applying his weight to it to prevent her from moving it further. Keeping his eyes on her pain-stricken face while continuing to grin, like he enjoyed watching her anguish, he reached down and forced the torn piece of fabric under her leg and pulled the two ends up on top, tying them into a tight knot against her thigh.

"That should help," Roger said, lifting his weight from her ankle. "You're lucky the old bitch missed the major artery, or you'd be dead already." Then, unexpectedly, he twisted himself around and plopped his body next to hers, sitting up against the glass to match her posture.

Sitting terrified next to him, her body still trembling uncontrollably, Sylvie's eyes shifted sideways to look at Roger peripherally to keep from turning her head.

"Why are you doing this?" she questioned, fighting back more tears.

She could hear Roger's tongue lap against his lips as he opened his mouth to speak.

"I thought we'd get to know a little about each other before the inevitable happened," he stated, a wheezing sound in his voice. "I mean, the *real* us," he added. "What can I say - I'm a gentleman who enjoys friendly conversation."

"A gentleman? Ha! I know all I need to know about you," Sylvie returned through quivering lips.

"Do you?" he replied. "Please tell. I'd love to hear all the nasty little details."

"I know you're a demented fuck pedophile who gets his jollies raping little kids and hurting people weaker than you," she seethed through closed teeth. "Well, here I am, fucker. Weak as you like it." Sylvie's anger and fear forced her to lash out. She hoped it would buy her some time. If she could keep him talking, maybe help would arrive.

"Yes, I do have that reputation, don't I? I blame my mother. She could have stopped what was happening when she found out what my baby-sitter was doing. That's what mothers are for. They're supposed to protect their babies. Instead, she let that woman do those awful things to me. Over and over again. But it wasn't as bad as you might think. I was only afraid in the beginning - when my babysitter first started playing those games with me. You get used to things pretty quickly. You become numb to it. Soon, I wasn't a scared little boy anymore. Tabitha taught me a lot during my young childhood. I don't blame her; everyone wants to be touched. Everyone wants to be loved."

"That wasn't love, you sick freak."

"Oh, but it was," he replied. "It was more love than my mother ever showed me. She's the true monster here. She's the one who made me who I am."

"People like you are all the same," Sylvie interjected, disgusted and having heard enough of his twisted fantasy. "You're always blaming other people for your fucked up lives. You're still that scared little boy, afraid to accept responsibility. Yes, it was repulsive and messed up that your mother let things go on as long as she did, but you got out of it, placed in a foster home with a family who loved you. You had a chance to make your life better. You had a chance to learn from the wrongs done to you. But then you went and fucked that up, too, when you raped your foster sister, you sick bastard. You made your choice."

Roger snorted at Sylvie's harsh words, silencing any further remarks from the frightened doctor. Sylvie felt his shoulder rub against hers as he took a deep breath, his chest raising and lowering as she tried to shift her upper body away from his.

"I loved my little foster sister," Roger grunted. "Lisa was such a sweet, young girl - and pretty too. She had a smile that could light up the room. I could never do anything to hurt her. Unfortunately, I was too young to stop her father from doing them."

Sylvie's eyes widened, and she partially turned her head in Roger's direction, staggered by his words. He glanced at her and then quickly turned his stare away.

"That's right," he continued. "I didn't rape my foster sister. It was her father. When I found out about it and threatened to tell, he dragged us both out into the shed and ordered me to beat her. When I refused, he forced me to watch as he did it. He beat the living hell out of Lisa. Standing over her slumped, battered body, he pointed his finger in my face and told me that if he could beat his daughter that badly, someone whom he loved, imagine how easy it would be for him to kill me, someone he didn't love at all. He walked out of that shed with one thought on his mind, leaving us both behind. Lisa was too injured to move; I was too afraid to. We were still in there twenty minutes later when the door burst open, a police officer standing behind my sobbing foster dad while he screamed, 'What have you done?'"

Sylvie's thoughts wandered. Greta thought *she* was a good actress; this fucker deserved an Academy Award for his performance.

"I didn't say anything to the police," Roger continued, "too fearful for my life. I knew Lisa was scared too, pointing at me when the police officer asked who had done that to her. I never condemned her for that. What little girl could rat out her father? I took the blame that day for something I hadn't done, and I've been paying for it ever since.

"I'm not a pedophile," he continued. "I've never raped anyone. Oh sure, I've thought about being with people, forcing myself upon them, thanks to my 'fucked up life,' as you called it. But I've never once acted on it."

"Bullshit," Sylvie let slip. "You're a fucking liar. Do you think I don't know your kind? Do you think I don't know *you*, Roger? What about that young intern at Teton you beat and were going to rape?"

Roger inhaled deeply, a gurgling noise coming from his chest. "Ah, yes," he responded. "The intern. I was wondering when that would come up again. I've already told you about her. I was only doing what they made me do."

"What *they* made you do?" Sylvie questioned. "Who? What the hell are you talking about?"

Roger huffed, mixed with a muted laugh. "I think it's time you learned the *real* truth."

He reached into his breast pocket and pulled out a small piece of paper crumpled in a ball. He rolled it in his fingertips before extending his hand toward Sylvie. She looked at his face, then the paper ball in his palm. Reluctantly, she slowly grabbed it from him and unraveled it.

She recognized what it was immediately. It was the torn fragment from the list of names she'd previously pulled from the filing cabinet. She read the remaining four names:

Clement St.Pierre
Greta Lambeau
Gertrude Landry
Olivia Wendell

Suddenly, her face became flushed. Her hands began to shake as she stared in shock.

"Recognize anyone?" Roger asked, a nasty smirk falling across his lips.

Chapter 32

We All Fall Down

It wasn't so much reading the names that left Sylvie speechless, although the shock of who was on the list reverberated within her brain. It was Roger's words, or perhaps, the way he said them like he knew something he wasn't supposed to know. Something he *couldn't* know. She was becoming paranoid.

"That's right," Roger said, nodding, his voice hoarse. "They were there too – Greta and Gertrude. That was a lifetime ago. But it was Dr. Prichard," he continued. "Him and his goddamn 'miracle drug.' It was supposed to make everything better. It was supposed to make *me* better.

"I was the first. I wanted the nasty thoughts to go away, to forget about the pain of my past. He promised me he could do that. Ditrolazipan Sulfate, the 'drug of the future,' he called it. It was supposed to make the subject highly suggestible. He thought he could make people's mental health disorders go away with just a few simple words. He didn't realize the drug overstimulated the subject's amygdala, increasing their level of anger and rage. I felt like a poor man's version of Jekyll and Hyde, as my calm self was smothered and suppressed by some darker side of me that took control of my actions. The worst part was that the rational side of me was always present, paralyzed and unable to do anything about it but watch through horrified eyes at what I was becoming.

"The drug worked, though. Just not in the way the demented doctor told me it would. It made me highly suggestible; that much was true. He could make me do things: stand motionless for an hour, scratch a non-existent itch until my skin was bloody and raw, run my hands under scalding hot water until they were blistery, and . . , other things.

"But the bad thoughts remained with me, and no matter how many different iterations of the drug I was administered, he couldn't expel them from my mind.

"He thought he was getting close to a breakthrough and wanted to test the limits of what he could get a patient to do. I had no idea he was such a sadistic prick. That's where the intern came in.

"I was given the newly formulated Ditrol-26 that morning. It threw me for a loop, almost knocking me out. I was in a daze most of the morning, not understanding where I was. But the words were clear, whispered to me while I lay half-unconscious, strapped to the bed. *'Hurt the girl, hurt the girl, hurt the girl.'*

"I remember waking in my room, the pretty young thing standing over me, holding a tray of food. I felt my blood instantly begin to boil as the words, *'hurt the girl'* screamed into my brain. I couldn't stop myself. Rage consumed me. I didn't want to do anything to her, but I was no longer in control. So, seeing her there in my room, I . . , well - you read the file. I'm sure you know the rest."

"So, Dr. Prichard told you to hurt the girl?"

"My dear, no; he only administered the drug. The whispers were from someone else."

"Who?"

"When the intern first arrived at Teton," Roger replied, "she was such a pretty girl. I wasn't the on-ly person who took notice. There was another who felt threatened by her beauty."

"Greta," Sylvie remarked, staring at the dead woman's body.

"Jealousy never looked good on that woman," Roger added. "She knew I was going through treatments with Dr. Prichard; we'd talked about it since she'd been through some treatments herself. She knew what it did to us; she knew what it did to *me*. When that intern started, Greta was no longer the one who held all the patients' attention. She was bitter and didn't like anyone stealing her spot-light. She knew Dr. Prichard had given me the Di-trol-26 that morning, and knowing he was looking for extreme results, she offered a solution. He let her come into the room where I lay helpless. He let her say those things to me. He knew if it worked, the blame couldn't fall on him. After all, it was a crazy woman who put those ideas in my head."

"That's what the fight you had with Greta in the past was all about, wasn't it?" Sylvie questioned.

"When I later found out it was her who whispered those things to me, I may have gotten a little rough with her. Nothing she didn't deserve."

Sylvie's eyes shifted from side to side, taking the man's words in. She didn't know what to believe. She knew he was dangerous; he just killed Greta right in front of her. Greta had done the same to Mrs. Landry. If Roger hadn't shown up, Greta would have killed her, too. She was sure Roger saved that pleasure for himself.

"Why are you telling me this?" Sylvie asked, the tears no longer flowing. "Why don't you just get it over with and kill me already?"

"Kill you?" he questioned. "I told you before, you have nothing to fear from me. But like before and throughout my entire life, nobody believes me. Everyone thinks I'm delusional, crazy, hysterical. Eh, some of that may be true. But I've said enough about my problems. Let's talk about you, shall we?"

"I don't have any problems," Sylvie replied, gritting her teeth, unwilling to give in to the sadistic man's lies.

"Oh? Then why are you here?"

"I'm here . . ," she paused, again looking at the list of names on the paper. "I'm here because I made a promise."

"To yourself?"

"No. To my parents."

"Now we're getting somewhere. Do tell."

Sylvie exhaled heavily, wondering why she was even indulging the sick man's request except to buy herself more time.

"I promised them I would take care of something. Unfortunately, I don't think it's going to happen now."

"Well, that's too bad," Roger stated, licking his lips. "But I still think you can do it."

Sylvie shook her head, sneering. "You don't get it; you have no idea what I came here to do."

"But I do," he replied. "I know exactly why you're here. I knew it from the day I laid eyes on you."

"You don't know shit, you crazy fuck," she remarked.

"It's funny, isn't it?" Roger said in a sly kind of voice. "You think you know a person. You thought you knew me. But you don't. Not really. I, however, most certainly know you."

Sylvie's heart skipped a beat. "What are you talking about?"

"Come now; did you honestly think I could forget that face? I told you, names come and go, but faces I rarely forget. You've aged since that time, but I make a habit of filing away the pretty ones in my head. It's a shame, though; you had such a lovely name. You shouldn't have gone through all the trouble just for me. But I do feel honored . . , Olivia."

Sylvie's eyes widened as she glanced at the last name on the list. Olivia Wendell. Daughter of Christopher Wendell and Gail Zcieveteveicz Wendell.

"How did you know it was me?" she asked, giving up on any further pretense.

"After what had happened, they told me all about you and the condition you were in before they transferred me to Somerset. I demanded it. After what I had done to you that day in my room, I was sickened. I beat you so badly; you were in the hospital for weeks. I couldn't get over the guilt."

Sylvie closed her eyes, trying to rid herself of the images of that day. "It was only my second day on the job. It wasn't supposed to be like that."

"No, it shouldn't have been. I'm so sorry for what I did to you - what *they* made me do to you."

Sylvie opened her eyes, shaking her head. "But wait, I don't understand. Why is my name on that list? It doesn't make any sense."

Roger inhaled through his nose, held it for a moment, and then released the breath accompanied by wheezing.

"Dr. Prichard said he'd take care of everything. He said he'd make you forget. He visited you in the hospital just after you'd woken. You had been through so much. I didn't want you to live with the images I had to endure. That was *my* torture to bear. I made him promise me you wouldn't remember anything that had happened."

"But I don't . . ." Sylvie stopped in mid-sentence, Roger's words evoking a memory she'd long since suppressed. She recalled how angry she was the day she awoke - how full of rage. The doctors had to subdue and restrain her to the bed. She assumed it was because of the news they'd delivered, but now, she knew it was more.

What did the doctor do to me, Sylvie wondered. She was beginning to believe Roger's words.

"When I saw you walk through these doors for the first time," Roger continued, "I knew Dr. Prichard didn't do what he'd promised me."

"I think he did," Sylvie said. "I didn't remember anything about what had happened to me at Teton until years later, when the nightmares began, and the memories flooded back to me."

Roger grunted. "I wish it would have lasted. That's the thing about trauma; you can't escape it. I've been trying to escape mine my whole life."

Sylvie dipped her chin, rubbing her leg just above her stab wound. "You said you recognized me from the start. Do the others..."

"They don't know jack shit."

"If you knew, why didn't you say anything?"

"If I did, you would've been dead a year ago. Greta would have made sure of it. It's like I told you; I've seen how this all plays out. It's been repeating over and over in my head for two decades. The question is, do you have it in you to do what you came here to do? Can you keep your promise to your parents?"

"My . . .parents." A single tear escaped from Sylvie's eye as she glanced at the bloody knife on the floor beside Greta's hand, only inches from her own foot. She felt her jaw tighten. "You destroyed everything. The doctors told me the news when I woke up. My parents were on the way to the hospital after they found out what had happened. They shouldn't have been out. They should have been home. But because of *you* – because of what you did to me...

"My father was always such a careful driver, always looking both ways even after the light turned green to ensure the cross-traffic had stopped. But that day, his mind was so preoccupied with getting to the hospital to see me that he never saw the truck running the red.

"Can you imagine, waking up in the hospital, not knowing why you're there, and being told your parents were dead, killed in a car accident on their way to see you? I was eighteen years old, and my whole world had just ended in a flash."

Sylvie whipped her head in Roger's direction.

"*You* did that to me, you son of a bitch."

Roger snickered at her choice of words. "You know my story, Sylvie. I *am* a son of a bitch. She was an awful bitch, at that. I told you before," he continued, staring into her eyes, "there's a worse fate in store for me." His stare shifted to the knife by her foot then back to meet her eyes. "Do what you must."

Sylvie turned her head slightly to spot the knife in her peripheral vision. When she focused back on Roger, he offered an accepting nod.

Ignoring the pain in her leg, Sylvie twisted onto her right side and stretched forward, grabbing for the knife barely within her reach. It was a struggle, with her leg on fire and every fiber of her being screaming at her. She grabbed the knife and twisted back to an upright position, pointing the blade at the sorrowful-looking man.

"Do you know how long I've waited for this moment?" Sylvie remarked, her eyes burning with anger. "I wasn't sure I'd ever get the opportunity. But then those two bitches made it possible." She swung the knife sideways, pointing at the two dead women, before swinging it back to Roger. "I should just kill you." Her hand began to tremble as she fought with her conscience.

"Remember what I told you," Roger began, a subtle smile forming on his lips. "I can't stop what's coming, just as you can't stop what's coming. I can't live with it anymore, Sylvie, and you shouldn't have to."

Just then, Sylvie recalled the words she had spoken to Tremont.

Inside every bad person, there's some good.

Roger showed he had a good side, after all, saving Sylvie from certain death at the hands of Greta. It was time for her to return the favor.

Just as inside every good person, there's some bad.

She lunged forward, plunging the knife into Roger's stomach, burying it up to the handle. Staring into his cold eyes while he gasped, Sylvie twisted the knife sideways and yanked it out, watching his body jerk. He didn't deserve to be set free while she remained, burdened with her tragic story, but she had to do it for her own sanity.

She sat beside him, the man who took everything from her, emotionless, while he slowly expired. She did it. She did what she set out to do. She closed her eyes and dropped her chin to her chest, weak, exhausted, bloody. Within the silence, she heard the distant sirens blaring louder as they came closer. Kevin had gotten help. She was saved – her life, if not her soul.

What she'd done, killing Roger, she wasn't afraid of the consequences. She knew how everything looked. Kevin was a witness. He'd seen Greta with the knife. He'd seen Roger kill Greta with the broken broom handle. She was going to be all right. Legally, at least.

Sylvie closed her eyes to calm her troubled thoughts before the authorities arrived. When she'd started her new job as Sylvie Zcieveteveicz, legally changing it using her middle name "Sylvie," and her mother's maiden name, "Zcieveteveicz," all she could think about was keeping her promise and getting out of that place. She'd now kept that promise, but she wasn't ready to leave just yet. She realized now her job wasn't done.

Roger committed the act against her, and for that, he paid the price. But there were two others. Greta, the woman who whispered the order, was already dead, the opportunity to exact revenge sadly taken from Sylvie when Roger shoved a broomstick through her chest. The other . . , the one who came to her in her nightmares, always a shadowy silhouette, whispering to her in the darkness. She now knew who the whispers belonged to. The faceless image in her mind stepped from the shadows to reveal himself, the man who haunted her since she was eighteen years old in that hospital bed. It was Dr. Prichard, the true "bad man."

She'd once wondered who would tell her story. With that same lingering thought in her mind, Sylvie opened her eyes and smiled.

And outside, the rain began to fall.

A LETTER FROM THE AUTHOR

Dear readers,

I hope you loved *Just Listen*, and if you did, I'd be very grateful if you'd consider writing a review. I love to hear what readers think, which helps me grow as an author, and it makes such a difference in helping new readers discover my books for the first time.

Check out my website at:

javo-publication.square.site, where copies of all of my books (including signed copies) can be purchased. You can also find them on Amazon.

Thank you so much!

Jeff

YOU'RE NEXT ON THE LIST

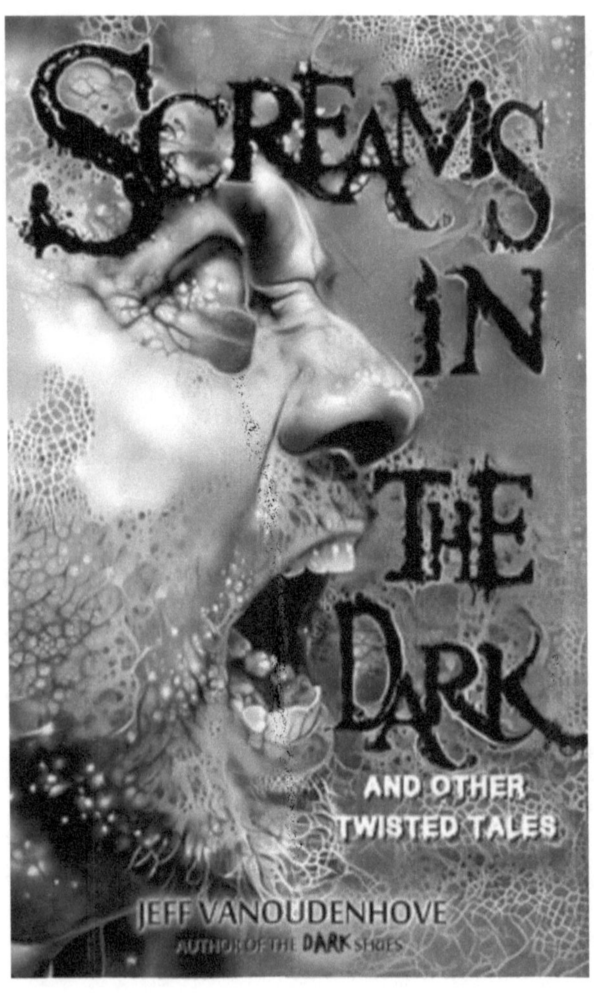

Screams
In
The
Dark
AND OTHER
TWISTED TALES
JEFF VANOUDENHOVE
AUTHOR OF THE DARK SHOES

DARK PLACE
FIRST IN THE DARK SERIES
JEFF VANOUDENHOVE

SOMETHING SINISTER AWAITS

WITNESS THE RISE OF EVIL

DARK
QUEEN
TH3RD
IN THE
DARK
SERIES
JEFF VANOUDENHOVE

HELL IS FOR CHILDREN

THE END IS NEAR

Jeff VanOudenhove has written several novels in the genre of dark fiction, including the **Dark Series** and the psychological suspense thriller, **The Alphabet Killer**. His talent for storytelling combines unforgettable characters and dire situations, mixed with astonishing plot twists. **Just Listen** is Jeff's eighth book. He lives in Western Massachusetts with his wife.